*Stigmata of Bliss*

THE
SEAGULL
LIBRARY OF
GERMAN
LITERATURE

KLAUS MERZ

*Stigmata of Bliss*

THREE NOVELLAS

TRANSLATED BY TESS LEWIS

LONDON  NEW YORK  CALCUTTA

This publication was supported by a grant from the Goethe-Institut India

swiss arts council
prʊhelvetia

The original English publication of this book was supported
by a grant from Pro Helvetia, Swiss Arts Council

**Seagull Books, 2021**

ISBN   978 0 8574 2 838 7

**British Library Cataloguing-in-Publication Data**
A catalogue record for this book is available from the British Library

Typeset by Seagull Books, Calcutta, India
Printed and bound by WordsWorth India, New Delhi, India

# CONTENTS

*Jacob Asleep*

*Evenings you see him roam,*
*as if walking were a repose*
*in the light that keeps the world's treasures*
*secure*
*out in the open.*

From the poem 'Fragment' by Erika Burkart

1

CHILD RENZ. Dust motes whirl from the window-sill. Behind me stands the cross, rotten at the base, its slender copper roof mantled with a gossamer film of verdigris. I learnt to read from the nine letters burnt into the crosspiece.

My older brother died at birth and should, in fact, have been named Jacob. But since there was no baptism, our parents, uncharacteristically compliant, insisted on observing their first child's official anonymity.

Holding my father's hand, holding my mother's hand, between my grandparents' black winter coats, I spelt out again and again my brother's strange designation. Child Renz.

The adults' tears at his graveside gradually grew less frequent, as did our visits to the cemetery.—The young couple's wedding portrait, in which the shadow of an early pregnancy must have been visible in the bride's face, never stood on our parlour buffet.

Begonias alternated with pansies, pansies with geraniums, the rosebush lasted longest, until one day the weather-beaten cross ended up in the woodshed next to the pigsty and no one in the family quite knew what to do with it.

A decade later, it was probably passed on, together with all other moveable items and the firewood supply, along with the workbench and dented petrol canister, chopping block and old motorcycle tyres, to the new owners of the property, which then changed hands a second time not long after, before it was finally levelled.

I hunch inwardly to keep from banging my head against the beam of the empty stall as I did back then, the day I broke open the piggy bank filled with fifty-rappen pieces in the sty's semi-darkness, and the scene plays itself out again in my mind.

The coins burnt in my small fist, they scorched themselves into my palm and I suddenly understood what grown-ups meant when they claimed that money cannot buy happiness.

To cover up my crime, I scattered the metal discs, warmed by my hand, in a high arc over the freshly fallen snow and I prayed ardently to Jacob, that he would, for heaven's sake, make them all disappear.

After the snowmelt, the silver pieces glinted mercilessly in the sun once again. I gathered them up, horrified.

*Bad Lukas*, Father said.

He stood with his birch broom in hand, looking down at me from the corrugated-iron roof of the flour storehouse, on which some of the coins had landed.

*Damn Jacob!* I thought.

As always, a ruffled sparrow squatted in the sand of the burnt-out aviary.

2

The birds' screams were heard all the way over in the next village. Wings alight, the exotic creatures flapped around the cage while Grandfather, the garden hose in one hand and an axe in the other, simultaneously doused and slaughtered as the siren from the town below steadily drew near.

A headless laughing kookaburra flew over the garden fence onto the train tracks, where the linesman later found it lying between the rusty ties.

The arsonist was never caught. Grandfather let the birds stay. Day in, day out, their creaky oaths annoyed the neighbours no end.

One of the two aviaries later became our sandbox. There we made baguettes and Bundt cakes, built castles and a fortress, and dug our way to the centre of the earth.

And after Sunday school we let loose the Great Flood.

The other enormous cage, near the south side of the house, was turned into a bower. On the flower-patterned camp bed, under the mocha-brown camel-hair blanket from Sharm el-Sheik, a birthday present from Franz, Father, dusty and tired after the nightshift, took his afternoon naps from spring until autumn.

The walls of the extension were painted yellow. One rested there as if inside an egg. Mother drew the curtains for Father, her climbing roses twined dutifully along the fascia board. On the cover-strip over the head of the garden bed was a row of grease spots, one next to the other, a venial bit of untidiness in the leafy shadows, the deposits of Father's pink wax earplugs.

One afternoon Father returned to the bakery from the bower, pale and unsteady, the camelhair blanket wrapped around his shoulders, as if returning from battle.

Half-asleep, he had fallen into an ambush. The doctors called it epilepsy.

3

In the half-light of the large aviary, Sonja and I dove into our realm of love as silver-grey de Havilland Vampires roared overhead, flying low on their way back to base. We slipped our fingers between each other's toes, then sniffed them until, light-headed, we dropped off to sleep.

Sonja's three brothers guarded our love nest while her father stood outside the saddlery and fed his carding machine with horsehair that also sprouted, thick and black, from under the neckline of his shirt.

In the summer, he refinished sagging mattresses— flowered, striped and mottled—from all over the region and let us use the stained ticking for our teepees. Sedge grass smouldered on the campfire and kept the horseflies away.

During the winter months, we rode through the dirty workshop on the damaged saddles of the local manufacturers' families or crouched like silent natives, drunk on glue fumes, in the dusky leather storeroom. On this evening, however, Sonja's brothers, as neglectful of their duties as they often seemed in daytime, had fallen asleep over their hunting spears and our parents carried us off to bed.

Their path led past the former fishpond. After Grandfather's carp-breeding phase, which had seamlessly followed his bird phase, the pond had become our wading pool.

The surface of the water had looked like the sequinned costume of a white clown when Grandfather's carp shed their scales and floated naked, bellyup, across the concrete-lined basin towards the drain.

One stormy night in April, streams had overflowed their beds, entire houses were flooded, potatoes swam out of cellar windows, fallen pine branches split the railway's overhead wires in two and one end landed in the nearby fish pond. DO NOT TOUCH! warned the yellow signs with their black skull-and-crossbones grinning down from every electrical pole. We did not lay a finger on the dead fish.

On cloudless summer days, our spruced-up inland sea with its vitriol-blue water lightened the leaden weight of my younger brother's bones.

He lay stretched out in the pond, a black inner tube around his chest, a cork disc like a halo supporting his head and he was very frightened when we shot our air guns over his stomach at the magpies in Mother's salad beds.

Sometimes the newts' red bellies flashed over the drainpipe and startled him. Water striders grabbed him with their long, thin legs or a fire salamander burnt his white skin.

In our family, we called my brother Sunny.

He didn't scream when the red tabby lay next to him in the water. I had drowned it to release him from the rage he could never let loose on us. Nor I on him.

We called our love bower *Orient*.

4

*Franz, light your hand on fire and make it shine for us!*

In a moment of distraction while playing the game in which he jabbed the point of his knife fast as a drum roll here and there between his outspread fingers, Franz had already lost one digit, the smallest. Since then, he much preferred to set his 'damaged goods', as he called his hand, on fire.

He poured petrol over his skin and ignited it with a lighter. We were frightened and we laughed. He laughed with us and quickly shoved his blazing fingers into the pocket of his blue overalls to smother the flames and at the same time pulled a burning cigarette from his left ear. The saddler's boys were amazed.

Anyone who had never seen Franz walk on his hands through our woodshed, who had never yet been struck by the sight of the mermaid wrapping her ink-blue arms around Franz's shin as she swam slowly upwards beneath his rolled-up trouser legs, was not one of the initiated.

Nor would he find space on the seat of Franz's Harley Davidson, which Franz wheeled out of the workshop's shadows and into the sunlight on good days so that we, the bravest and the heaviest, could be freed from gravity's pull on the motorcycle's large seat.

Those were stigmata of bliss that adorned our calves and ankles when we could no longer resist centrifugal forces on the long, sweeping curves behind Wynon's cheese dairy and our bare flesh pressed against the scorching exhaust pipe.

Only back at home did our bliss turn to agony and our wounds smoulder. Our parents smeared butter on our burns and strictly forbade us those wild rides.

5

Behind his broad back reigned a dark void that smelt of leather. Asphalt and turf shot past my bare, bony knees. The manhole covers gleamed. The thirty-two-year-old steering the heavy motorcycle was my father.

The landscape into which we drove pulsed like an open fontanel. It glowed red at the edges. A drunken farmer drove his Ford straight at us. Father veered onto the field and braked. Milk spilt from the open trunk of the car as it zigzagged along the road.

We almost got away that time, I said to Father. Something about that sentences seemed wrong, but he didn't correct me. He lifted me from the seat and hugged me to his chest. We breathed deeply and sat on the short grass next to the idling machine.

Hydrocephalus. A round, hairy, legless insect the size of a fully laden hay cart came towards us across the moraine. We got back on the motorcycle and drove off.

I tried to picture my younger brother, whose head, they told me, was growing too fast. Alarmed by this excess, we raced down into the valley. In panic and titanic, we grew much too fast in the quickly falling twilight. The lights of the canton's capital city all lit up at once.

My brother was sleeping when we entered the room. His small, modelled head lay on the white pillow and knew nothing of itself. Nor did I see what I knew. Only later would ever-helpful life teach us the expression 'water on the brain'.

I turned towards Mother's bed. She lay in a puddle of pain and reached for me with her hand. I did not take off my leather pilot helmet. Despair slowly filled the room with electricity, our eyes shone green. The small bundle awoke:

*Together*
*we shall carry him*
*aslant through this world*, Father said.

When we returned home, the laundry woman was still standing at her ironing board, starching our collars.

6

We only used the second floor of our house to sleep when we were ill or on major holidays. We spent the rest of our time on the ground floor: in the bakery, in the kitchen, in the shop and in the small parlour adjacent to it with frost patterns on the windows.

In summer, red geraniums stood on the windowsill, bursting with health. They were the fruit of Mother's green thumb. The plants stood for the other side of her life, green and red and abundant. Whatever she touched set down roots, bloomed, bore fruit and brought a radiance to her dull eyes that faded again only with the chrysanthemums.

Father stubbornly insisted on calling our little parlour the *office*, because in the far corner of this small room stood his desk with the blue ledger in the top drawer along with old bills and receipts.

His desk served as a repository for our clothes, letters, printed matter and schoolboy odds and ends. Dust settled between the erasers, the tweezers for Grandmother's chin hair, the paper clips and pencils.

We sat around the extending table or lay on the worn sofa, listening to the programmes broadcast over the radio transmitter in Beromünster, holding our ears close to the speaker so as to not disturb the customers on the other side of the door we always left ajar.

Occasionally we were joined by the man who delivered the flour, coated with dust, and the men who delivered chocolate or eggs. Sometimes Mother spread out before us the beautiful hand-woven cloth brought by a soft-spoken salesman from the north-west of Switzerland. And she came alive. With the coins she had saved from her housekeeping money, she decorated the house and expanded our Christmas finery with an additional pillow, a tablecloth or the chestnut red of new curtains. And in the evening, she helped Father put on an exquisite tie he liked but rarely wore, pastel-coloured, with no lustre but full of warmth.

In the office, unexpected visitors were fobbed off with mountains of treats. Relatives and friends collided head first with sweet dumplings. Black tea spiked with Spanish wine was offered as an accompaniment.

*I simply can't tolerate the combination*, our aunt Mrs Brettschneider said and served herself straight from the bottle. She gave the tea and dumplings to her grandchildren. She talked with her hands, stained brown with tobacco juice. The fastest cigar roller in the area, she talked rapidly too, pattering as fast as a machine gun.

And yet, words caught even in her throat the day Franz staggered in with the Blaupunkt. He had bought this Cadillac of radios for us from some bankrupt estate and was translating the announcements of Radio Luxembourg before he'd even plugged it in and set it on the table.

Behind the beige fabric cover, we could vaguely make out the loudspeaker's vacuum tubes, and the transmitter keys reminded the egg delivery man of Franz's harmonium with its ivory keyboard. At the top of his voice he declared that now even people whose fingers were too short would be able to make music. Franz swatted his hand away from the buttons and read out the radio stations of Europe as if reciting a poem.

With his left hand he turned the frequency dial in search of a station. Only then did he swing open the appliance's cranium with a brisk tug. Inside the box a gramophone was spinning. Franz had also brought a record.

*Brunswik* was written on the black disc, it had to be another word for happiness. The parlour floor rocked. The black trumpeter's hoarse singing drove Mrs Brettschneider and her three grandchildren instantly from the office and we scooted closer together.

*On the sunny side of the street.*

*All those who want to walk in joy*, we heard our aunt warbling a folk song as she left.

Only after night fell did we gather again to listen to the news broadcast from Beromünster. Long after our neighbours had begun their treks to *Laramie*, we hung on the echo of trusted voices:

Of Theodor H. from London,

Hans O. from Paris,

Heiner G. from New York.

Their inflections shaped our conceptions of the great wide world, of distant cities and conflicts, and their influence would endure. Franz squeezed the bridge of his nose with thumb and forefinger.

*So I can hear you better*, he said and tossed back a pill. Against the travel bug and pain.

Given his long, uneventful mornings, my little brother Sunny was the first to lose his heart, little by little, to the shortwave.

In order to hear the latest hits and the explosive American—and German—rock 'n' roll, which sometimes almost had him jumping out of his chair, he would even put up with our northern neighbour's vacuum-cleaner commercials.

But all this happened only long after Grandmother had given up the battle against her chin hair once and for all and become a faith healer.

## 7

After the birds and the fish, Grandfather was determined to keep bees: *You must eat honey, children,* he told us. *I'll make it for you.*

Grandfather built himself an insect paradise near the cemetery. He soon grew immune to their stings. He mixed sugar water, changed the honeycombs, removed the dead bees from the hives' entrances and greeted the queens. When a colony swarmed, he would dive into his personal fountain of youth. He spread honey on his shaven head and brought the renegades home as a buzzing crown.

*The queen also has a stinger but she only uses it to prevail or perish in duels with a rival. The drones, in contrast, are defenceless and die when evicted from the hive once their time is up,* Grandfather explained to our apprentice baker as if reading him the riot act, before scraping off the honey as he did every spring and autumn.

Wherever you put your hand, there you stuck. Now and again a bee flew into someone's mouth and he had to be taken to the emergency room. In the evening, the liquid gold stood in pots and jars on the pastry table as a defence against hard winters. As soon as I was old enough to go to school and therefore out into the world, Grandfather advised me that I would weather hard winters best with slices of bread and honey and his blue army coat.

The stiff cloth was immediately removed from the bindle in which it had been stored with mothballs and unrolled. Brettschneider, the Austrian who had married into the family and, as a tailor, fully lived up to his name, took my measurements. The grown-ups insisted he keep the epaulets, silver buttons and the large belt buckle with a pointed mordant.

I stood like a mummy in Brettschneider's fitting room. Legs crossed, he sat perched like a demon on his sewing table, from his thin neck hung a faded measuring tape with which he could hang me at any time.

My mother, also increasingly unhappy, began fussing helplessly over her child soldier in the rough blue cloth. Flies buzzed around our heads.

*Es steht ein Soldat am Wolgastrand*, Brettschneider sang in a quavering voice and smugly looked over his basted seams.

A snowstorm set in, twilight fell on the battlefield, the tailor's workshop darkened.

In my distress—and following family tradition—
I held my breath. Before long, the imperial maneuvers
of our Austrian in-law and his allies, the Swiss bee-
keeper and constable baker, were dispelled.

They promised me an anorak with a kangaroo
pouch for the coming winter. I took a breath. Mother
hugged me. We did not let go of each other again for
the rest of the day.

8

*Rise and walk*! Grandmother said to my younger
brother every morning. She balanced on her left foot
and raised her arthritic hands to the ceiling in invoca-
tion. Our windowpanes trembled as the eight-o'clock
train, empty boxcar in tow, shot past our house and into
the valley.

My brother raised his head on her command and
rocked back and forth a bit at the table. The effort made
a vein in his forehead swell ominously and after a while
he collapsed back into his chair. The morning news
drowned out the healer's deep sighs.

Determined to make every last effort, Grandmother
summoned her brothers and sisters to prayer shortly
before Christmas. Under the dark murmuring of

the palefaces who had come running to her call from the Lazarus Chapel, our parlour table slowly rose from the ground before our eyes. My brother, however, remained seated.

We assured our dismayed parents, who had stepped out only briefly for a breath of fresh air during these most demanding days of the year and had crossed paths with the hooded horde in black snowshoes on their own doorstep, that we hadn't suffered any harm in the exercise. Grandmother admitted defeat.

*If it works, it works.*

*If it doesn't work, it still works*, she said and was almost back to her old self, but then decided to return to the unheated chapel with her holy troops after all. Enraged, Father yanked one of the inner window frames off its hinges and smashed it onto the train tracks outside.

Mother wept.


We tallied the accounts. I was always responsible for the copper and nickel coins and I stacked the five, ten and twenty rappen pieces into high towers. Mother was in charge of the silver coins. Father's job was easiest. His few bills were soon counted.

On the last day of each month, he prepared his employees' pay packets, dark yellow envelopes with glue strips. If there was too little money in the drawer, mother helped pay the salaries with her savings.

The journeymen seemed to glow from within when, after knocking respectfully on the parlour door, they signed their names on the pay slip carefully, ceremoniously and even a bit audaciously, as if writing with melted chocolate on an iced cake, while the maids usually became self-conscious when they held Father's fountain pen and were relieved when it was all done.

Father always added an extra fünfliber coin. That was his way.

Mother attributed this to his illness.

9

In our family, illness had priority over all else. After Grandmother walked barefoot through the snow in her religious frenzy and, weightless as old, brittle leaves, was carried out of the house with the first spring storms, my brother was once again the most seriously ill member of the family, so ill that people gladly came often to visit him. Out on the street, everyone, young and old, turned to stare. They tripped over kerbstones, caught their trousers and skirts on the garden fences and knocked their gaping heads on telegraph poles when I pushed him along the road in his high-wheeled cart.

There were only a few television shows at the time and the tabloids were still restrained, so, live and in real time, we satisfied some of the local craving for entertainment.

On our best days, when inner despair suddenly tipped into boundless self-confidence, we mercilessly called these idiots exactly as we saw them and we chased after them with pointed laughter and the front wheels of our heavy cart spinning in the air.

The highpoint of our involuntary showmanship was certainly Father's *grand mal* seizure on the sidewalk. On a Sunday morning stroll, he fell to the ground in the village centre. As if on command, the good Samaritans came out of their homes and built a cathedral of curious bodies around us.

Sunny was stuck in the dark chancel and watched helplessly from his cart. Pale, I knelt down next to my convulsing father and ministered as best I could to the sharp chimes of acrid exhalations.

After an eternity, which transformed my brother and me into two wizened old men—the sun was at its zenith and the smell of burnt meat hung in the air— Father came to and looked around. He nodded at me, got up slowly and took up where he had left off.

He straightened his clothes, blew his nose in his Sunday handkerchief, pulled his dark blue beret down over his forehead and focused his eyes on a distant point on the horizon.

He took hold of my brother's cabriolet and put his arm around my shoulders. Without deigning to give the dumbfounded Sunday team another glance, we walked out of a dark tunnel into the brightest afternoon I had ever known.

10

That evening I was struck with fever. Heigh-ho, how the beads of mercury rolled merrily over my feather duvet and dove quickly between the white sheets when yet another thermometer broke in my damp hands. And how long Mother stayed in my room, searching for the lost silvery treasure in my bed and in the cracks of the plank flooring.

When she was gone, I peeled off the vinegar-soaked socks and hearkened again to Jacob:

*Are you sleeping, are you sleeping,*
*Brother Jacob, Brother Jacob?*

I sang softly to the panelled ceiling.

We had learnt that canon in kindergarten and had sung it in as many as three voices. I immediately knew whom it was about. The kindergarten teacher was secretly on my side. Without her, Jacob would never have awakened for me.

When the mercury in the thermometer rose past 102 degrees and I chanted his canon, Jacob pushed aside the heavy curtain that covered the window facing the train tracks and stood near me. He was almost a head taller than I was and had long hair. But he was nothing like an angel. He was my brother, after all.

*I heard the bells* was all he said and sat down on my bed. He knew that I couldn't sleep, couldn't even close my eyes to the inflamed world.

On the far side of the 102-degree mark, Jacob brushed his hands over my eyes and regularly took over my duties. I was immediately freed of my worries and soon got better.

On the morning after Jacob's last appearance at my bedside, the bike with the electric motor stood by our door. I caressed its silver-grey cylinders and pushed the bicycle at a run. With the breadbasket on my back and free of fever for less than a day, I swung myself onto the seat and after just a few yards let Mother's misgivings scatter in my slipstream.

11

I delivered bread to the old-age home, twelve lightly baked baguettes for their ruined teeth. I held my breath in the hallway with the deathbeds standing ready so I wouldn't get infected. Damp plaster plopped down from the ceiling. I galloped out of the hospice on the apprentice cook's apron strings. He gazed at my new wheels with reverence and awe.

I then made a beeline for the delivery entrances of the inns. Even though I now arrived motorized, my face no longer flushed beet-red with exertion, the waitresses still only treated me to a large glass of Negerschweiss. This cola with the dark continent on the label along with the Cape of Good Hope, the 'Cape of Storms which Bartolomeu Dias was the first European to round in 1487, gave me strength to finish my own rounds.

In a high arc, I peed against the tall, gilded garden gate before entering the villa of the local deities, Nägel & Stahl, to deliver their Bircher-Benner health bread.

The empty breadbasket turned upside down on my back for sleeker aerodynamics and my head lowered between the cables on the handlebars, I hurtled down to the valley. And bolder than ever before, I braked up short near the girls.

No one wore helmets in those days. On the curves, I scraped the asphalt with my pedals so that sparks flew. Once I rammed my shoulder into a flagpole and its loose cable cut a bleeding gash across my skull.

Father helped with the shaving and stitches and fainted at our doctor's feet only at the eighteenth stitch, when it was almost all done.

We left the emergency room together, each of us wearing a white turban.

Fortunately my motorized bicycle was unscathed.

## 12

When Sunny was a few months old, they drilled two holes in the back of his head to keep his skull from growing too quickly. Against the light, you could see his heart beating under his scraggly hair.

Sunny reached up with his short arm, put his small hand on his head, one finger on the pulsing spot and laughed when I called him 'Two-Stroke'.

We each had our auxiliary engine.

This equipment kept us alive.


The gardener's daughter waited for the Sunday bread in the shade of the rubber trees. I entered the greenhouse through the back door and scared her with my bandaged head.

We compared our middle-class worries and then fell silent, tongues touching, until the glass panes around us clouded over with steam.

It smelt of peat.


Only *The Bells of Our Homeland* on the garden nursery's radio called us back home. It was Saturday evening, the middle classes were bathing before listening to the weekly radio play.

For a while I called myself Paul Cox after the police commissioner in the radio dramas. Then the commissioners' names changed more and more often. As did the seasoned foreign correspondents I had always thought were irreplaceable and everlasting. Not even Victor W. in Rome, the eternal city, was able to stick it out.

Nevertheless we remained true to these invisible spirits of the airwaves and every Saturday sat at the parlour table until the late news.

As the national anthem faded away, Mother was already scooping the steaming egg noodles from the boiling water. These noodles, garnished with just a dash of liquid seasoning, were our midnight feast. We ate like kings, only without meat or servants.

This weekly communion was our family conspiracy, guarded by Sunny, asleep upstairs.

I drank the wine from Father's glass.


Before we went to bed, we gathered at the window. When I was lucky, Sputnik passed us with its load of monkeys. Still, the warning lights on the nearby radio tower flashed reliably in the southern sky. We felt like we were looking at a large star sign. Father always looked for the Great Dipper and for Orion in the winter months. Mother sniffed at a sprig of lavender.

## 13

When we left the *office*, our eyes fell on the large naked man in the oil painting next to the parlour door, Father's boldest acquisition in years: art for bread.

He was fond of the painter, born the same year he was, who strode into the shop in trousers spotted with paint and pointed at the darkest loaf with a rainbow under his fingernails.

His broadest brush in one hand, a rag that happens to double as a loincloth in the other, the painter in the self-portrait stands facing his reflection in a mirror. The summer heat turns the light yellow in his studio in the old hayloft, as it does our oil painting.

Gary Cooper stands in the same posture in the hot town square of Hadleyville, waiting for the noon train. But he is wearing clothes and a sheriff's badge on his lapel. Alone and ready, even though he has no actual duties. That's his way.

We watched the movie one Sunday afternoon. After the final shoot-out between Kane and Frank Miller we set off for home without a word, our eyes dry as dust, and with a rolling gait we left the ghost town behind. It was the same gait as Father's when, after an eternity, he finally got up from the ground and we headed out of the dark tunnel into the light and homewards.

At home Father mixed the yeast starter and Mother combed the ricochet shots from my hair.

Even though you can't see them, the painter's feet are planted firmly on the ground. He is a solid man, observing himself closely and curiously under our gaze. Below his moustache, a thin mouth.

The painter must have stepped out of his picture and up to the canvas hundreds of times. Squinting, he took his own measure with his outstretched hand and painted.

Everyone should be able to stand like that, Father had said and taken the nail from between his lips and hammered it into the wall to hang the picture. For once, he brooked no contradiction.

For me it's a matter of applying colours. For you it's a matter of daily bread.

Father agreed.

14

When I couldn't sleep after events like the Sunday afternoon Western, I made sure to ask about Lot's wife who had been discussed in Sunday school again that morning.

I simply couldn't understand why God unleashed destruction so mercilessly on Sodom and Gomorrah. He didn't even spare the children. More than that, I did not understand why he turned Lot's wife into a pillar of salt when all she did was look back. How could God do this to men and women when he loves mankind? It was a question that got Father going no matter how tired he was.

*Yes, that's the way the world works and always has,* he'd say. *The hardest-hearted imbeciles, the hypocrites and arse-kissers, the truly inhuman are the ones who survive unscathed—the most ruthless, in fact. Those who don't take the slightest notice of what's going on behind their backs. The ones who don't have the guts to look back. The ones who are fine with any catastrophe as long as they're promised they'll survive.*

*Hats off to Lot's wife, hats off,* he said as he began pacing back and forth excitedly and breathing feverishly. Mother watched him apprehensively.

*Tell your teachers that this woman should be praised even though she isn't even given a name in the books.*

*Tell them that Lot's wife is the only one who turned around, despite the terrible threats, when she heard what was going on behind her.*

*When she heard the thunder, the screams, and flashes of lightning threw the shadows of those who'd taken to their heels onto the ground in front of her.*

*When she felt the heat from the fire raging behind her.*

*Tell your teacher that Lot's wife is the only one who turned against the stream of the fleeing crowd, her face a mask of horror and her limbs frozen with fear at the sight of such cruelty and fury. And tell your catechism teacher that we saw Gary Cooper, saw him cross the town square alone. In Hadleyville.*

*And that another such man hangs on our wall at home, naked.*

*Tell her that, and now go to sleep!*

15

Why Sonya ended up marrying the cattle dealer of all people, in whose household she'd done an apprenticeship after graduating from high school, always remained a mystery to us.

The widower had devoted barely two weeks to mourning his first wife after she died in childbirth of a thrombosis when rumours of Sonya's imminent marriage reached us.

Under our half-hearted shower of rice and along a cordon of black umbrellas, the cattle dealer led his young bride into a furious snowstorm and out of our village for good. *It's no good omen*, my mother declared, *Sonya marrying this man on the anniversary of Franz's death.*

After this precipitous alliance and the resulting whispers, we pictured Sonya ever-more often standing atop her silo in eastern Switzerland.

So very young, suffering from homesickness and dejected in way she had never been as a child, she must have gazed from the silo roof towards the canton of Jura, her eyes slowly grazing the old hillsides which she sensed more than saw.

She kept watch like this for years, stoically, as the cattle dealer's children grew up around her, until one evening she finally dove head-first onto the paving stones and the animals in the stable broke out of their stalls.

From that day on, the cattle dealer abandoned himself even more passionately to his racehorses that never won. It was his turn soon after when, small and thin as he'd always been, he was racing his own sulky and was struck full in the head by one of the horses' hind hooves and became feebleminded.

Sonya had left his half-grown children a latticed wooden box. Filled with grey cocoons. It was November.

Four months later the butterflies emerged:

Large tortoiseshells.

Swallowtails.

Not a mourning cloak among them.

16

Exactly seven years to the day before Sonya's wedding, news that Franz, Father's brother was dead reached us in the office. A few years earlier, he had finally emigrated to Alaska, but then had crashed a plane in a forest nearby.

He had always worn hats, played the harmonium with nine fingers, recited poems and suffered from constant headaches.

He could do magic tricks and ride heavy motorcycles. And fly planes.

We never tore the page of the day he died from the calendar.


The newspaper reported that a single-engine model CAP 10B aeroplane had crashed in a forest not far from T. Franz and his companion from Fort Yukon died on the spot.

The plane, witnesses claimed, had been stolen from Z. twenty minutes before the crash and took off in a particularly daredevil manner. The plane flew directly to T., where the self-proclaimed pilot cut the engines and circled over his hometown, steadily losing altitude.

The pilot had veered to the left and tried to regain altitude, but could not avoid the trees, according to three foresters.

The manoeuvres reported by the witnesses led the investigators to conclude that the inadequately skilled pilot had not given the flight his full attention as he circled above his own neighbourhood.

Franz was buried at the southern end of the cemetery. His girlfriend's ashes were shipped back to Alaska.

Father did not touch Franz's inheritance. A scrawny bailiff wheeled the old Harley out of our woodshed. As forfeit for the wrecked plane.

The next day, Father heard the faint sound of a harmonium coming from Franz's grave, as if the instrument had secretly joined Franz under the ground.

The 8th of May 1945, when Franz's playing in the Blue Elephant kept the whole town dancing until the early hours, was a day seared into the memories of all who were there.

Just before daybreak, with the help of a few musicians from the military band and some hard-drinking air-raid wardens, the black case had been hauled up to a windowsill on the third floor of the inn. Following the organist's advice, they filled the bellows with water to increase the explosive effect of this peace bomb.

With a muffled crash, the dripping harmonium shattered on the town square right next to the pharmacy to the applause of the assembled peace commando.

There was hardly a family in the entire area that did not acquire over the course of the day an ivory relic or at least a damp shard of wood to commemorate the peace accords.

Sonya's father unfolded his chequered handkerchief as he stood at Franz's grave.

*OW* was embroidered on it. The cloth was as big as a parachute.

He blew his nose in it.

The Federal Office of Topology's grey aeroplane circled above the mourners.

17

On his twentieth birthday, Franz had crossed the Sankt Gotthard Pass on foot when he returned home from temporary exile from his family before emigrating for the first time to Alaska, where he spat ice cubes, listened to his powerful stream of urine shattering on the frozen ground and shared fish with his two Eskimo wives.

It was also on the bank of the Yukon river that he lay on the ground with a crushed foot after a hunting expedition until a bear dragged him back to camp through the ice and snow.

Franz often recounted these stories to a rapt and eager audience in our office on his brief returns from the icy wastes of Alaska until the employees began to shiver and Grandfather's rage at his wayward son cooled and the men in the group urgently needed a schnapps to warm up.

It was Franz who first called my younger brother *Sunny* and did so without leaving me in the shade.

I left the small room and sat under the cuckoo clock at the end of the corridor and weighed the two metal pinecones in my hands. The clock stopped.

What I wanted most was to hurl the iron weights through the window of the veranda onto the train tracks in order to settle my account with time once and for all. Then I felt the last warmth from the bread oven rise in me through the flooring. It made my grief for Franz almost habitable.

I let the weights drop.

After Franz died, Father no longer had a brother to take care of or who took care of him. All he had left was us, his emergency guard, who surrounded him epileptically when he had an attack. We waited, pale and impatient, for him to return. We turned my brother to face the wall so that he would not suffer too.

Sometimes Father laughed as soon as he got up again. He pretended nothing had happened. Or snarled at us like a wounded animal.

If I did not hear him snoring on the nights that followed, I would creep into my parents' room and hold my ear to his mouth to make sure he was breathing.

Mother, also awake, would take me by the hand and lead me through the Christmas room, past Father's books and her black piano, along the grey cloud of upholstered furniture and back to bed.

In the light of dark moons that shone through her white nightdress, I went back to sleep.

18

The hardest times for us were the relatively painless ones. We could not endure the latency of new wounds and immediately turned to the suffering of others, which was still much more difficult for us bear than our own misery.

As precaution, we cut our fingers, spilt hot water on our thighs, broke a collarbone or a rib. We offered sacrifices to the painless periods, hoping to prolong them with these minor skirmishes, extending the time before something more serious happened again and Mother, pale, lips pressed tight, her hair gone white, returned from a clinic our customers had recommended to us in good faith where her deepening melancholy could be treated.

Father and I had taken her to the sanatorium against her feeble resistance.

*Let's go* is all she said when we loaded her suitcases into the car weeks later and she didn't look back once at the stork of a nurse who monitored us with tilted head from the doorway of the clinic as Mother was discharged.

The first thing Mother did at home was to get rid of the electric blanket that had always warmed her bed.

And she adamantly refused to let us replace it with a better one.

For fear of electric shocks.


If you follow her rose beds, you reach the southern tip of her narrow garden. There I planted two trees with Grandfather, a poplar when Sunny was born and, somewhat delayed, an already stately linden tree for me.

We hardly said a word as we dug up the earth, rammed supporting poles into the ground, tied the cords and hauled buckets of water.

The poplar was chopped down three decades later by the allotment's subsequent owner, probably at the behest of the Swiss railways, which, from its earliest days, had run our Orient Express through this steep, unprofitable stretch of land directly along our garden fence.


The felling of the tree must have coincided almost exactly with my brother's death. We had a sun chiselled into his tombstone and left enough space below his name for those of our parents. They settled in next to him a few years later.


One clear, starry January night, I set them on Orion's belt, Father's favourite constellation in the winter skies with Sunny between them. They dangled their legs in the emptiness of the universe. And were not afraid.

I could not place Jacob with them because he's asleep in his hiding place.


19


My linden tree still stands. Its powerful limbs grab at the dead wires over the abandoned tracks. Cattails grow between the ties, the rails have lost their gleam, no inspector paces the line with small steps and a red warning flag in a quiver on his back. And there's no one to hand the weather-beaten employee a cream pastry through the kitchen window.

He would bite his worn teeth so hard into the pastry, the vanilla cream would always squirt out onto the brown gravel. Him, from the railways, and us, his meagre catering crew at the side of this steep stretch.


On afternoons when there was no school, I carried our family's heavy sunshine up the almost insurmountable steps and into a third-class compartment.

My brother sat up straight next to me on the wooden bench and his eyes, peering out from under his heavy brow, watched the landscape roll by. Travelling made us weightless. We never forgot that he couldn't walk. But driving, flying, singing—all that was possible.

We put one over on the mundane force of gravity and grinned as we passed our anxious parental home in a secret victory parade along the well-controlled railway line.

When the light in the compartment turned pine green as we entered the ravine, my brother read aloud the signs announcing, in all three national languages, that throwing objects out of the window was strictly forbidden. A pair of enamel plaques was mounted on every wooden cornice. That was the moment to hurl the empty bottles I'd brought along in a blue duffel bag out of the window and into the stream. I hit the rock dead-on. Beside himself with delight, Sunny smacked his thighs with both hands, threw his head back, roaring with laughter, and began hyperventilating. I held my hand tight over his nose and mouth until he caught his breath with a snort.

Along this stretch, we had practised early on getting used to the failure of our common dreams: no matter how many stones we piled up on the tracks along with packages of sulphur we'd scraped from entire boxes of matches or the much more impressive carbide charges, in order to finally derail the train that thundered past us relentlessly, nothing ever happened that altered our daily routine—until one particularly loud explosion that frightened us too, put our young neighbour who lived above the kiosk right next to the tracks into early labour.

Leaning over the railing of her balcony, she screamed at us in despair. In our opinion, absolutely no one had the right to get this beautiful woman pregnant, least of all her accountant.

She bore him twins.


Our treasure must still lie buried between the tracks and the tree. The piece of stovepipe in which we'd hidden it must have rusted away long ago. Didn't we sign in blood?

And what was the exact wording of our first promise and oath? I no longer remember.

But we must have sensed, even then, that it was not in Rome, London or Paris, or even on the Beinwil-Beromünster stretch that we would stand the test of time, but only *in* or *under* the ground.

For we were aiming at nothing less than eternity and had a knight's helmet on our coat of arms in honour of noble ancestors or, perhaps unconsciously, as an emblem of time's passing.

We added the shed antler of a roebuck because we treasured it.

Adventurers, explorers, decipherers of the world's mysteries—*saviours* of a sort is what we wanted to be, Sonya, Sonya's brother, my own brother, parked backwards, and I.

Still, we later forced the engineer to take his foot off the dead man's pedal and swear bloody murder when, in high spirits or sheer bravery, we rested our heads on the rails until we could feel the rumbling of the approaching Orient Express deep inside, like wild labour pains.

20

A glance over my shoulder falls on the rooftop terrace and its coarse asphalt surface. Sunny sits in his oversize three-wheeler, turning in circles on my watch. I egg him on. Smoke rises from the laundry's high brick chimney, the slap of wet sheets reaches our ears along with scraps of an Italian folk song. Near the house, the home signal of the Orient Express has fallen back to its resting position, the railway crossing gates point back up at the clouds.

On the morning of my thirteenth birthday, one of my classmates had painted a full moon on the classroom's grey sky:

*It's your brother's head, the watermelon!* I stood blindly in the gales of laughter.

That afternoon, the smoke from the chimney drifted down onto the terrace.

*Floor it!*

My brother took me literally, gave it all he had, took the curve too tightly and fell onto the tar. He didn't scream because his breath had been knocked out of him as usual. I felt relief as an explosion of accumulated rage flared up and beat against my red interior walls, but in the same moment I was shaken, stunned with sorrow and immediately knelt down next to my wounded brother and blew air into his lungs through his nose, pressed my handkerchief against the scrapes along the edges of his forehead.

Our parents rushed up and carried him, unconscious, into the house. They locked the door of the parlour with its Christmas finery against me and the outside world.

As if the hard work were nothing to her, Marietta stood next to the wood-fired water heater and hauled one white sheet after the other over the basin's edge. I sought refuge under her wings. Marietta had come to us from her southern homeland twelve years after the end of the war to earn enough for a new eye. Those who stood to her right were besotted with her beauty. Those who changed sides were aghast at the devastation in her young face.—A startled soldier had shot the child's eye out just before the end of the war. Since then her face was divided between her mutilated Catholic side and her proud Roman side. During the May Devotions to the Blessed Virgin Mary, to which, as a little Protestant, I was occasionally allowed to accompany her, she usually kept her good eye closed and I could worship her undisturbed. When my parents weren't home, I would confess my sins in her lap.

*Alfa*, I whispered when she called me her Romeo.

My mother's relations with her southern employee were as divided as Marietta's young face. My mother trusted the injured side completely and would have gladly placed her hand gently on it every day to heal it or at least to comfort the girl. She never got used to the disturbing side of Marietta's face, however—she was, herself, not much older—and she often and decisively announced her deep loathing for the *one-sided* seductiveness that had all our male employees in her thrall.

Mother no doubt also feared for my innocence, since she once turned up when I lay in Marietta's garret, playing the wolf. I'd eaten some chalk and the squeaking of my voice alarmed her. Mother stood in the doorway as Marietta was absent-mindedly operating on me to remove the seven young kids from my shorts.

I never experienced a fairy tale that intimately again and ever since that afternoon, I've been convinced that true happiness is wordless and ephemeral.

Later, at Marietta's request, I shaved her underarms and, week after week, soaped up her soft calves. We had discovered our own America.

It was probably a mistake for me, of all people, to dissuade her from bleaching her black hair straw-blond.

Across the counter, a customer translated the letter from Sicily a stunned Marietta had handed to us.

Someone had been found on the outskirts of Agrigento who would take Marietta even with her bad eye. The expense could, therefore, be saved and her seven months' salary be brought home in a pouch. Marietta left.

Only her bad eye remained dry.

When my photographs of Marietta's departure were developed, I asked our photographer, who, under his black cloth, had already managed to make my brother and me look like two angels, to paint a healthy eye into one picture taken before Marietta had time to turn the good side of her face towards the camera.

With diluted India ink and his finest paintbrush, he finally released the pain trapped in Marietta's face.

That picture I kept for myself.

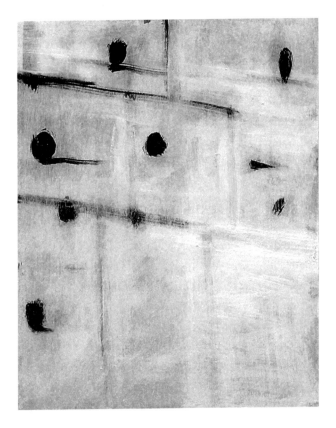

## 21

*All those who wish to walk in joy,*
*Know Dill's sells the best clothes for man and boy.*

With these trenchant verses, the new clothier in town took his decisive revenge on Brettschneider, who decided, under the pressure of this new competition, to move back to Vorarlberg with his brash wife—which was fine with me. I knew, furthermore, that this successful clothier had brazenly been compensated not just at Brettschneider's expense, but also Emanuel Geibel's (1815–54).

Regli had made us memorize all the poems by Geibel in the blue songbook. This substitute teacher, long past the age of retirement, had wanted to teach us something that would last. He even taught us the songs' melodies, although he was only a German teacher and always sang off-key.

It was this same Regli who had promised me new shock absorbers and he kept his word after I carried him on my moped's baggage rack up to the old-age home right before a storm broke one sweltering summer afternoon.

I had finished a long tour through the village and was hanging around the station when Regli limped off the train. I offered him a ride.

There was no more bread for me to deliver since Father had switched from 'breadcrumbs' to 'utilities' shortly before his forty-fifth birthday. He stopped in at every household in our village and, with a finely sharpened pencil, conscientiously recorded everyone's water and electricity consumption in his black book.

In order to finally free himself from the night shifts that sparked his illness, he'd reluctantly but calmly abandoned his 'daily bread', as he still called it, to go 'door-to-door'.

Only straight talk, he claimed, and the irritation in the eyes of the electricity consumers enabled him to find his own way through his extensive new clientele's middling pretensions—and to keep his soul intact.

After some time, even his supervisor, an emaciated, carping technocrat from the town in the valley began to look at the 'failure' from Obersteg with new eyes and some respect.

Along with dog biscuits, an eraser, cigarettes, his emergency dose of medicine and extra pencils, Father always kept a flashlight in his coat pockets. A headlamp would have been more practical when making his way through the dark crawl spaces, stairwells, cellar alcoves, corners draped with cobwebs and stinking lavatories to reach the black meters.

Father probably wanted to protect us from the already ever-present threat of ridicule and so renounced the cyclopic gear for our sakes.

## 22

The doctor had fumbled around roughly and clumsily in my mother's wide-open pudenda and broken the healthy baby's neck at birth. With his metal forceps.

Father never shied from direct talk with me either whenever I had time—which was more and more seldom—to leave my moped and accompany him on his rounds in the outskirts, all the way out to the isolated farms with their watchdogs on chains and open cesspits. On those rounds, I would ask him questions.

Before answering, Father would pick up a pebble and compare it to the moon's pitted skull. Or he would point out the damp native strain of wheat that could not make decent bread flour without the addition of imported varieties, something the farmers never liked hearing.

Then he pointed out over the field. On the far edge stood an abandoned substation, a baroque tower with a red tile roof.

*Rapunzel, Rapunzel,* he used to call out to the tower back when his profession had nothing to do with electricity.

*Rapunzel, Rapunzel, let down your hair!*

He never had to wait long before the window under the rusty eaves opened a crack and my mother's beautiful young face appeared in the weathered window frame.

They had found the key to the tower in the knee-high grass one Ascension Day right after the procession, with its dragging prayers and balking horses, colourful baldachins and corpulent priests had passed the substation house. They'd climbed the stairs to the isolators, current transformers and star connections in the narrow tower chamber. And as the sun set, they gave off enough energy to power the entire village.

As visible proof of their love, a light burnt in every single house in the area, Father told me.

For a moment I saw the young couple's silhouettes illuminated by Father's words in a way I could never have pictured my schoolmates' parents.

Yet, embarrassed, Father was already wiping the fleeting glow of his words from his forehead to return to the inexorable darkening of Mother's soul. She had probably given up her struggle with the angel deep inside her long before Jacob's birth.

*Maybe even already on our last walk home from the substation*, Father said. *When she was certain she was pregnant.*

In my memory, Jacob's cross still leans against the wood stacks as tall as a man in the shed, exactly as it had been placed back then and never removed.

If someday someone somewhere happens on the cross with the nine letters on the crosspiece: It belongs to me.

*A Man's Fate*

In memoriam K.B.

*[Storytelling] does not aim to convey the pure
essence of the thing, like information or a report.
It sinks the thing into the life of the storyteller, in
order to bring it out of him again. Thus traces of
the storyteller cling to the story the way the hand-
prints of the potter cling to the clay vessel.*

Walter Benjamin, 'The Storyteller'

We had searched for you, called your name, dug. But
the rescue crews all returned to the valley empty-
handed. The helicopters landed without results, their
tanks were refilled and they stood ready for other
duties. Nor was there any response when your picture
was broadcast on television. Without exception, the
clairvoyants all led us astray. There was nothing left to
do but follow our hunches. The possibility that you
might have gone to ground in the Caribbean was never
taken seriously, not for you, not for us. There was no
movement in your bank accounts.

'My Thaler lost his way.' We clung your wife's phrase, as did your silent children, and after all the fruitless searches we gradually resumed our familiar daily routines without you.—You only returned in dreams. You came into our living rooms and bedrooms as if nothing had happened and you sat at our tables, you lay down in your bed. Until we secretly begged you to stay wherever it is you are now.

Under the high blanket of autumn fog, the neighbourhood houses huddle in a pack, not like wolves but
rather like sheep, given their timid demeanour. The
apartment buildings' flat roofs are still boldest. Otherwise, there is only despondency under the small
pointed gables.

After Fanny and Herta, two other storm fronts
whose names have already been forgotten rumbled
over the land. A young man barks his morning poem
into the microphone as if he were a Newfoundland.
Thaler turns off the radio and reaches for his briefcase.
He leaves the tattered copy of Störig's *Small World
History of Philosophy* behind on the table.

When Thaler steps through the door, he pulls himself together. The neighbourhood children have all
been in day care and school for some time now. Or
they've already begun their apprenticeships to become
like us. Only the postman, with his bundles of junk
post, circles through the rain-dampened town like an
inveterate bearer of hope.

The car park's three buildings were freshly re-plastered
this summer. And since then, a neon column bearing
the famous carmaker's name and logo stands on the
street corner to call the region's attention even more
insistently to the ever-ready king of cars. Digitally and
for free, passers-by are offered the temperature and the

exact time to take along on their way. Every day, the postman resets his watch in front of the petrol station, his prime meridian lies somewhere between lead-free and diesel.

In mid-September two cars collided a few metres past the car park. One of the drivers came away with a few injuries, the other died at the scene of the accident. Since that day fresh flowers on the side of the road recall the man's sudden, pointless death. Particularly on foggy days this sad marker also reminds Thaler of the south where these kinds of untamed memorials have a long tradition and the light is brighter than it is here.

A boy stops by the flowers next to the gas station. He's wearing an olive-green army coat and hangs his helmet on his moped's handlebar. The lanky teen stands on the side of the road, indecisive and self-conscious, or as if he had something unseemly in mind. From the corner of his eye, he watches the speeding cars and motorcycles accelerate just before the town-limit sign and roar past him. In the nearby shop windows, the same old pieces of furniture slumber.

When the boy tears his eyes away from the road and turns back towards the spot on the kerb in memory of his dead father and, looking down at the grass, closes his eyes for a moment, the golden sergeant's insignia on his sleeve flashes. Thaler has already crossed paths with the boy on his daily walks to school three times.

Today, Thaler is not heading to school. He is on his way to the internist, but first he wants to eat a smoked sausage in the outdoor cafe because the sun has pierced the fog. From his table—knife and fork already set out—his glance falls on the stone cross standing by the side of the road: Jesus is missing. Only his hands, his feet and his exposed heart rise in relief from the stone crossbeams. Neatly arranged, implements of torture and tools for crucifixion offer imaginative assistance for bona fides. Thaler takes a bite of bread.

Between the Cross Inn and the crucifix at the well, a rider and his horse stop for water. The animal almost drains the trough; a little girl is lifted up onto the saddle; the rider orders a beer at the bar. A convertible rounds the garden fence. The driver and his passengers are taking the sky's momentary clearing seriously. A bass beat thuds from their speakers.

Thaler has to summon some strong mustard to cut the sausage. One night, recently, someone seems to have left a rhinoceros in Thaler's belly, a rhino made of stone. And here Thaler already is, cup in hand to pass water. His blood flows warm, the doctor is friendly. It's still winter in the small Segantini print over the examination table.—Behind the glass front of the building next door, a young man, strapped into a fitness machine, lifts weights. Thaler bares his chest too. Between two machines, he waits for his X-ray: 'Why bother with a loincloth? Hand me a helmet!'

At the end of the second week in November, the light, bright and merciless, flickers under Thaler's heavy lids, shoots into his brain, warms his back, pulls at his toes.

For days now, his tongue has been lying like a dead animal in his mouth, its greenish surface making a Chinese healer enquire after the most frequent cause of death in his family.—What can he say? When he opens his mouth, what he wants to do most is vomit. And once again the word 'butcher bird' was stuck in his head as he made his way through a less-than-pleasant night: from three in the morning on, he is usually caught in a nightmare's clutches. Thaler curls into a ball, flips from his stomach to his back, pictures himself locked in a monkey cage, naked and holding a banana. The students from his school stand in front of the cage and laugh. Thaler wakes in the acrid dawn, drenched in sweat and his head on fire.

Honey and three lemons for a snack—in the morning, his knapsack is soon packed and he's off. Water can be found everywhere in the mountains. Thaler sits briefly at his desk, prints out the text he sweated over for so long, takes the manuscript from the printer and slips it next to the lemons in his knapsack.

*I visited Mother twice more after they moved her to hospice. In the late afternoon and again in the early evening —between the two, a storm broke, lifting manhole covers and uprooting trees.*

*The slim woman, barely sixty years old, hadn't got back on her feet after a minor operation. And because she adamantly refused all nourishment, they fed her through a tube and kept watch over her for weeks. Aside from her lack of will to live, the doctors could find no explanation for her steady deterioration. The wounds from the operation had long since healed.*

As Thaler steps out of the door and onto the flagstone path in his hiking boots, slighter and even more slender due to his self-imposed regimen, his children and their playmates stand in a silent guard of honour. The neighbour turns to her oleander and calls her cat. A long-haul jet measures out the deep-blue sky with its drone and soon disappears again behind the Finsterwald hill.

A heating-oil delivery man pulls up. The driver in the green-and-yellow truck brakes abruptly and asks the postman where he can find the oil tank for the newly built row houses. The postman shows him with a few hand gestures.—If heating-oil is being delivered on Saturdays, it means winter will soon be here. The postman checks his left wrist for the date and time.

As always, the reformed pastor sits at window in the Eintracht, his favourite bar, and looks out over his missing congregation. The church authorities decided, in order to cut costs, to join his parish to the neighbouring one, complete with its fanatical 'Counter-Reformer'. Since then the local pastor no longer preaches any sermons. If he does speak, it's to order another drink. *Amen.*

Thaler could buy himself a tent any day. A combination of party hut, igloo and knight's castle. For company events, birthday celebrations, barbeques. Against rain and snow. Winter and summer, the fabric shelter stands at the side of the road with a sign offering itself to rent to passersby, constantly reminding Thaler that he's neither particularly adventuresome nor sociable.

Perhaps, though, he would have felt sociable and been open to renting such a tent if the one by the side of the bicycle lane weren't also put to other uses, housing a series of alternating, competing special offers: for the cheese of the month; for a call to vote against the Swiss People's Party; for inexpensive 'discontinued' furniture. Thaler pictures the tables and chairs as fluid: a table like a walnut puddle for the eat-in kitchen, an oak-veneer fishpond in the bedroom and, under the rubber tree, a chaise longue that disappears into the horizon.

Light rain is forecast for the evening. Farmers spread their slurry over the fields. Winter grain bristles its frail fur. Today would have been Thaler's father's birthday. 'Washing and Drying. Steam-cleaning included' reads a sign above the car wash. 'It's all Gugelhopf' is the baker's current slogan. Thaler believes him. He always buys from this baker, Thaler likes his raisin buns best. And the baker never lies, even if he claimed as recently as yesterday that he was a Berliner.

On the bridge Thaler crosses briskly, a young woman, a friend of his, was hit by a falling swan. She had been knocked against the railing but was unhurt. The swan, a three-year old bird, died on the spot. It had got caught in the newly installed garlands of Christmas lights as it flew upstream.

The city administration, attacked immediately and fiercely, still insists on keeping their new lighting concept. To make an omelette you have to break some eggs, the Swiss People's Party representative apparently told the irate animal rights activists.

Thaler continues past the garden with the enormous pumpkins left to rot, the bloated corpses of the squash have turned black over the course of the past week. A pall lies over the field as if in the aftermath of a long, grim battle. Only here and there do a few colourful fruit glow from the furrows. The touch healer's grey Mercedes is parked in front of the half-timbered house. A rumour has been spreading that the healer sometimes lays his entire body weight on this or that client, with great success. If he ever has to brake suddenly, chances are good that he will be slain by his own emergency medical kit which he keeps on the rear dashboard.

'Sahara' is the name of the young woman at the cash register in the store on the opposite side of the street. Thaler had to spell out the nametag above Sahara's left breast twice before he believed her name the same as the desert. Since then while buying groceries he sometimes gazes over her black, pinned-up hair, past her dark, almond-shaped eyes, and imagines he sees sand lying between the stocked shelves.

A desert wind rises in the dried-fruit aisle. Soon, the store detective will call a red alert and at his command the customers will pull the red paper bags over their heads against the sandstorm without complaint. In a blind, endless caravan, they wind their way out of the sand-drift-covered store.

In front of the store a girl fills her shopping bag with colourful leaves.

Still this is not the time to stop and tarry but to make a bee-line to the train station. Krogtal, single ticket. Second class. The ticket machine reads 'malfunction' but there's no one there to turn to. So Thaler will travel without a ticket to the central train station and validate his ticket there. He can worry about the return ticket later.

Since the man retired, a cloud of fumes has wafted after him. Thaler knows him by sight. 'What's the destination?' the man asks Thaler as he passes and glances up with a sharp, measuring look. 'I can go wherever I like, it doesn't have to be Interlaken,' the retiree says, making a cheerful face. 'With a senior travel card, the borders are my only limit. Otherwise everything is permitted. Today, for example, I'm going to Gänsbrunnen for a quick Jura tour. Kettenjura. Tafeljura. The pressing-iron company. I can turn on the steam when I want!—No, my wife is not coming with me. You just go ahead, she says from the doorway with a white dust rag in her hand. A gesture of peace.'

Thaler wants to leave too, but the old man won't let him pull away. 'On the day I retired, I set up my headquarters up in the station cafe, the table for two near the door. The railway men always say hello when they see me sitting there. They know I've got things in mind, that I'm planning a trip. And the waitresses can gauge how hungry and thirsty I am from my eyes, their sensible shoes squeak: to your health, Mr Herrmann, you've got the life! They hit the nail on the head. In four hours I can be in Chiasso—what more could you possibly want? Walk across the border for a Chianti, *Denominazione di Origine Controllata*, as provisions for the trip home. The customs officers raise their fingers to their hat brims.—I've got a crossword-puzzle book in my left pocket, a passion of mine. And the best defence against being ambushed by *questions about the meaning of it all*. You know what I mean. Appenzeller bitters when you get to the Gotthard Pass. I usually know what I need to know. I can spot trashy books now and then, my fellow travellers' faces give them away. Their opinion of me ages their faces—young curmudgeon, I think in response and unexpectedly hit on the ten-letter word that had been escaping me. That's how life works on my puzzles for me day to day. I may let my subscription drop for next year and just solve everything from my headquarters. Have a safe trip!'

The long drive across Arizona years ago flashes before Thaler's eyes: 'Just take a nap!' his American friend had advised him after coffee and left Thaler alone with the newscaster's voice, going off to 'administer' to his new love, as he put it. A half-eaten pizza lies on the kitchen table. It's the size of a truck wheel. The tractor-trailers thunder past on the nearby highway.

Then the arrival of Thaler's girlfriend who had travelled to join him, their long descent into the Grand Canyon, their mute mutual desire, their chafing skin. And the subsequent escape from the tight quarters of the mobile home, from his lover's merciless embrace into the inhospitable landscape around them. Sweat. Thirst and loneliness were a way out and a catharsis, as he tried to explain later.

Back in the Old World, Thaler's friend from home takes his girlfriend to bed in an attempt to finally resolve the paralysing quarrel between her and Thaler and the two fall asleep. When Thaler finds them, he doesn't wake them up.

Thaler had only ever seen his parents so at ease together once, at an open-air celebration on the school-house square. The sparklers gave way to the Roman candles' volcanic shower of stars. The four of them sit together with other families at the long table and the music strikes up. The two boys hold bottles of sweet cider. Father bows and invites Mother to dance.

An indescribable glow lights up Mother's face after just a few turns. Father holds his back ramrod straight and charts his course with raised left hand. When Thaler turns his gaze away from his parents and lets it glide swiftly over those at his table, he sees the dancing couple reflected in their eyes too.—Until Father and Mother stumble over the kerb and end up lying in the flowerbed. Father is out of breath. His coronary vessels, as they should have known, are too narrow for English waltzes.

*Love Robert* is written in glittering letters over the black accordion's treble side. Thaler took refuge behind the orchestra podium after Father's fall. The dancers now glide across the floor as if on rails. Robert stands behind his powerful instrument, his arms bare, slowly unfolding his instrument then squeezing it back together. He spells out the lead melody on the black keyboard with his right hand, with his left he hits the bass notes as if he were standing behind a Stalin organ and launching rockets at the audience.

Thaler watches the fingers of the musical weight-lifter trapped in a cage of equipment and notices for the first time that the solo entertainer no longer has a single finger on his left hand. He pounds the bare stump on the mother of pearl buttons and produces a music that makes Thaler immediately forget the lack of digits and even himself. 'Waterproof, shock resistant, anti-magnetic' was engraved on the metal back of his first wristwatch. Thaler feels like his watch.

At midnight Robert sings and thunders 'I can't get no satisfaction' over the dance floor. The boys clap and cheer with excitement while those on the playground who are getting on in years finally air their discontent over this catastrophic music.

A drunk shouts 'Tom-bo-la!' incessantly into the celebration's din and throws his man-sized stuffed bear into the air. Robert gradually regains his strength and diverts his playing from his Rolling Stones adaptation back to an Austrian tune.

Thaler falls asleep on the edge of the lawn: he roller-skates up an increasingly steep street, his joy over his speed changing only very slowly into terror. A young woman whispers into his ear that someone is looking for him, Thaler grabs at her neck and holds on tight. The people sitting on the wooden benches have begun swaying to the music. At that point, his mother takes him gently by the hand because the family is heading home. Father is holding her other hand and is not saying a word. Thaler's brother follows at a short distance.

Thaler's brother is wearing a helmet. Like the racing cyclists on the track. But under the helmet he has no hair. An uncle brought him the helmet back from a six-day track race in Zürich-Oerlikon. So the brothers cycle together.

They leave the municipal border behind and fly over the land. Thaler lets his older brother win on the mountain. When they get off their bikes at the top of the pass, his brother looks at him mildly. 'I know perfectly well,' he says without a hint of reproach in his voice and buys a cheap cigar at the kiosk along with a condom to inflate.

With Father's pocketknife they cut the cheroot in equal halves. Hidden behind the crates of road salt, they smoke together before the ride down and burst the smoke filled condom in the air. 'Hiroshima!', Thaler's brother yells and swings into his saddle.

On the descent, Thaler has no chance against the fraternal projectile. At home he takes over the care of both budgies, the green and the blue, as agreed before his brother has to register again. For the next round of treatment.

*When I walked into the room around four in the afternoon, Mother was staring at the ceiling as usual and I didn't try to kiss her but held my ear to her mouth to see if she was still breathing. I sat on her bed and told her stories about her grandchildren's happy lives. Then I clasped her hand, which she passively let me take.*

*'Stop with your nonsense,' I said abruptly, 'please, stop already, enough!' And I started tickling the palm of Mother's hand so vigorously, that I myself started laughing uproariously with tears rolling down both cheeks as high walls of thunderclouds gathered outside and the light in the room darkened.*

*I pulled myself together, laid her white hand back on the coverlet and said goodbye, as I had been doing for weeks, with exactly the same words. To give us both a chance, I lingered a moment by double door each time, hoping that the vacant-eyed woman would one day turn her eyes towards me after all and call me back to her bedside as if nothing had happened.*

The teacher with the reddened face is wearing short socks. She holds up her right hand, as Karl Marx once had and as the large statue of the southern tip of Manhattan still does, and leads her throng of third graders across the platform between postbags, passers-by and train passengers. Thaler believes he sees a gleam in her face and in the children's eyes that is reflected softly here and there in the faces of those waiting on the platform like will-o'-the-wisps.

The children laugh, squint, sweat, drink from bottles, burp. Their knapsacks hang down to their knees and bounce along next to their shoes. They have jug ears and greasy hair but still look marvellous to Thaler. A chubby girl actually yodels. She doesn't notice the constant teasing from the boy in Coke-bottle glasses until he thumps her in the side and she scratches him back.

You cannot build a nation with children like these, Thaler thinks involuntarily. At least not in the way their topmost guardians occasionally envision when they attempt to plant market-driven thinking into the smallest heads, forgetting all the while that large, skewed, angular heads are also needed if there is still to be a place for thinking out and brooding upon what is large, lopsided and cumbrous.

Then in the train Thaler sits across from a man who does not sweat. Thaler is abashed in the face of his unfaltering perfection, the seat of his trousers, the scent of his aftershave, a planner, a man of action, a major business figure. He opens his laptop with a practised hand—and plays a card game on the screen. Once, when he looks up, Thaler momentarily sees a child sitting before him. From the third grade.

The candles on the tree have not been lit, still Thaler crouches on the staircase landing with a piece of beeswax in his hand on the first Christmas Eve after his father's death. His mother's calls and cajoling do not reach him. His brother's pleas bounce off him. Then he hears the fluttering songs from the living room, the wax in his hand slowly warms and softens.

Under the tree, Thaler see the red, two-seater pedal car that will earn back respect throughout the neighbourhood for the fatherless boys and their mother. Their godfather from Vaduz had the cabriolet sent by train, with seats made of real leather, with parking lights and low-beam headlights.—On St Stephen's Day the two boys drive around the schoolyard and the other children almost envy them their father's death. Whoever pays five rappen can go for one ride in the car.

When his older brother dies of a brain tumour three Christmases later, Thaler goes into the forest looking for wild animals. In the underbrush he finds an antler shed by a roe deer. He takes it as a sign and a distinction. When he wraps his fingers around it in the worn pocket of his trousers, it gives him strength.

He goes into the underbrush only after his walk through the fields and meadows, his loud calls over the furrows and turf have been in vain. No deer, no hare far and wide. The local hunting society had got there before him as usual and had already swept the hunting grounds clear with horns and beaters and lead shot. But he represents the wildlife's side, he would have liked to watch the animals, to count them and warn them. His Agfa Isolette camera with retractable bellows dangles from his neck. For pictures of wildlife and the forest.

Under one of his pictures, Thaler wrote 'High Escapes', which pleases him, even if his photographs mostly show fields or forests. As for the animals he photographed, no mere mortal's eye can detect them, he alone always knows where the animals can be found.

The mere sight of the timid animals always electrifies him anew. Perhaps he's addicted, addicted to deer and hares, mad for foxes. But this autumn day is not his day. Thaler photographs himself with the self-timer and is already reaching for his bicycle to return home when a little bunny appears at the top of the hill. Thaler leans into the pedals and quickens his pursuit. Yet the fleeing animal seems to have been abandoned by all benevolent spirits, seems to have suddenly forgotten all its tricks and wiles, it flees very nicely in a straight line as if on tracks laid along the field path—and so gives his pursuer a chance. Inside, Thaler is hot for the hunt, he cheers, wheezes, sweats. Then the little hare springs straight into the air, less than five metres from his front wheel. And the animal falls dead at his feet. Its heart stopped.

It's as if the air has been sucked out of the hollow. Thaler lets his bicycle drop into the grass and kneels down next to the dead animal. Once again he has stepped over the edge of life. And is gasping for breath. But his dismay about the hare—the dead, the frightened-to-death-yet-incarnate hare—quickly turns to a strange, even indecent joy: the inapproachable wilderness had never taken him so seriously before. Thaler photographs his animal and strokes its warm fur repeatedly with his fingertips. Then he makes a bed in the grass for the dead hare.

From his boyhood room, Thaler can see into the cells of the district prison. He can see the series of prisoners awaiting trial sitting away their days, heads in their hands or pacing restlessly back and forth. Four steps from the window to the door, from the door to the window four steps. And they beat their fists and the wall, beat themselves on the forehead. He wants to wave to them. Night falls. The light in the cells blinds the prisoners.

An old scout who is serving a sentence for a car accident and drink-driving is the first to teach Thaler the Morse code: SOS, . . . - - - . . . Thaler gets it right away, of course, as every child does. Thaler grabs the handbook for help and diligently memorizes the entire Morse alphabet. During the day they use their wash-cloths as flags, at night they stick to their pocket lamps.

Want to go home, the prisoner signals.

I too am alone, Thaler signals back.


With a leather ball in hand, Thaler stands at the dusty edge of the playing field, he had set down his schoolbag so he could play too. He steps rather awkwardly onto the grass and senses that all these darlings of their mothers and fathers, this entire brood of brothers and sisters had not been waiting for him. As always, he retreats to the goalpost before he is even told to, with all the consequences that ensue for the goalie: loneli-ness, fear of public failure, fear of having to leap into the midst of kicking football cleats.

Beyond that, however, Thaler also knows the craving for a penalty kick and the chance to withstand the pressure on the field, completely alone with just his hands and feet. For Thaler, the goalie is the most clearly defined position on the whole pitch. And when the surge rolls upfield, Sunday reigns in his white rectangle. No more danger, no more mob—even if the goalie ultimately always has the mob against him, even his own mob.

Chronic headaches have plagued Thaler since his brother's death. When others catch on to his constant consumption of aspirin, he fixes on glasses with dark frames as an antidote. They help him remain in the shadows somewhat, behind plastic and glass, and they ease his pain, which, in truth, he felt more in his chest than in his head.—The glasses also shield him tolerably well from his schoolmates' punches to the face and turn him into a reader. They both make him lonely and surround him with a crowd of dependable friends who share everything with him and understand him.

A large part of his teachers up until then, Thaler realizes, were not readers and didn't care at all for the doubt, the thoughtfulness, the questions and the imagination they believed they should always demand from their students. They simply cling with both hands to their sweat-stained lesson books.

Later, Thaler too will give lessons. Language and culture, philosophy: Plato's allegory of the cave. The students hear and see their teacher lecture and reason, like a shadow. It's like he's behind a pane of glass, they say when the headmaster asks them companionably for feedback and then asks them to be more precise so as to have something concrete to use when assigning classes. Denunciation, Thaler thinks to himself but continues toiling in the 'mines' until it is suggested to him that he should expand his horizons a bit—and he himself has to admit that the world, even those closest to him, often seem separated from him by a sheet of glass. Like that fish in the Berlin zoo that he had never forgotten, it resembled a child's head with fins and doleful eyes, lips opening and closing but no one could hear.

In an early, solitary decision, Thaler reached, as a young man, for the word 'philosophy'. As if for a star. He began to study literature too. Thaler walked through the mountains with Lenz, felt the tremors of the earthquake in Chile and the new sorrows of young W.

On a kibbutz he learnt how to juggle oranges and his love for a Jewish woman lured him for a while to the strictures of the Old Testament. But a series of abhorrent attacks and pitiless reprisals on-site took Thaler's breath away. He took to his heels and from then on he mistrusted religion and turned instead to sports, team sports. It was no replacement for brother, father or girlfriend. And what philosophy holds in store for him does not nourish him properly either.

'It seems to him there are a thousand bars and behind those thousand bars no world.' Such lines pierce Thaler like a friendly knife. He travels to Paris, goes straight to the Jardin des Plantes—there is no panther cage there any more. Instead, Thaler sees only cheerful *flâneurs* and mothers with children shaping snowballs from the first meagre snowfall and watching their colourful kites rise into the sky.

In a bar on the rue d'Aboukir, a stranger lays her hand on Thaler's knee, lets her golden stiletto slip from her foot, and with her wet tongue, makes her lipstick gleam.

Was all this part of the 'Cutlery of Love' as one of his countrymen who had been living in Paris for some time put it in his most recent novel, Thaler asked the young woman—this wasn't, in fact, what he was looking for right here right now. The woman does not quite understand what he means and, after a last, half-hearted squeeze, she leaves him alone.

On his way through the city, Thaler meets a man in sandals in front of a hospital. Is he looking for Empedocles, the healer, the one who overthrew the monarch, the wandering soul, the man asks him and does not wait for an answer. 'I am Empedocles,' he says and, gesturing towards his bare feet that glow fiery red in the ankle-deep snow, laughs.

Later, neither philosophy nor literature feed the man Thaler had become in the meantime. With a wife, a child, a single-family home. He installs a satellite dish on the roof in order to bring the world into his living room, as they say, lays a water hose in his garden and watches himself watering his own lawn.

His wife comes home from her exhausting job, she has to supervise a bunch of underage delinquents with dark circles under their eyes. Thaler cools her feet with the water from the hose. Mallows shoot from the borders in the garden. They open their deep-red throats, show their glamorous sex for one day, then wilt.

Now and then the ground beneath Thaler's feet will bloom, a piece of music, a picture, obvious and irrefutable as dreams, take possession of him. Or he thinks himself as deeply as possible into his wife's being, listens attentively to her soft cry.—Thaler returns home with Bruegel's hunters, the fire is burning and rocks him into a hopeful sleep. But the very next day misery and an enormous flood of trivialities pour over him again through the satellite, the newspaper, the classroom. He feels trapped again. November.

A Chinese woman carries a large satellite dish on her back through Jinzhai County, a photograph caption claims in Thaler's daily newspaper. All that is visible of the woman are her trouser legs and shoes. The gap in prosperity between city and country has increased steeply; nevertheless, the Chinese farmers should still be better off after twenty-five years of economic reforms than they are. The photograph is meant to offer evidence.

Also visible in the photograph in Thaler's newspaper, apart from the huge metal dish, are a road still wet with rain, rice fields to the left and a row of trees to the right, and a pasture fence on the horizon. The photographer chose a central perspective. The painter Ferdinand Hodler called his painting with a very similar perspective *Autumn Evening*. There are a few more leaves on Hodler's road, the figure and the satellite dish are missing, and there was no need for reflective paint on the tree trunks a hundred or so years ago. But Hodler's view, in contrast to the day's photograph, projected a 'prospering' world into infinity and did not stop at the very first 'metal bowl'.

'SatAn' was written on the first satellite dish Thaler had seen on a single-family house in a decidedly Catholic region. There were no grounds for reproaching the Saviour in outer space or of reproaching the bold first consumers of timidity before certain names. And the business of peddling distant pictures had continued to take its course.

*A quarter of a year after the procedure, which we had secretly hoped would also bring about the patient's psychological recovery, it was decided, in order to reduce costs and the need for personnel and with the consent of her nearest of kin, to move her to the former isolation ward. They wanted to put her under the unobtrusive care of specially trained nurses, who had often been successful in the past in bringing back to life patients for whom there seemed to be no possible medical treatment left, simply through their discreet presence 'between the lines', as the dark-skinned nurse put it.*

Hoar frost coats the land, the light licks at its brocade edges. This autumn the trees dropped all their leaves at once. The main road runs like a silver band along the train tracks towards the horizon.—For a few moments tears blurred the sight of Thaler's wife whom he has left behind. After a brief hesitation, she let him go without a word—he can see her thinking, 'Maybe it will help.'

His train gathers speed. Nowhere does he feel as secure as in a train. Surrounded only by chance companions. He finds them to be the most reliable and he feels closest to them.

Travelling divests one. Like a lover. Like a lover who leaves unnoticed after making love to return to her own life, having washed up only cursorily yet unhurt. And safe elsewhere. Or like the woman in the window who writes down what she sees, day in, day out, when she looks out at her surroundings. The cedar in the garden at the base of which she buried her dog years before, the wooded hill, the local traffic. And who listened to her own heart. That was enough and provided her with the necessary support:

'I live centre stage,' she would say each time Thaler went to see her. 'The navel of the world is right here.'—He did not need to possess her and, much more importantly, he could not lose her.

Halfway through his train route, Thaler cuts the first lemon, takes a bite of its flesh followed by a spoonful of mixed-blossom honey. His diet to stave off his father's illness, his brother's death, his looming unemployment and inner misery, the greenish coating on his tongue. As always, he is betting on self-healing with asceticism, tugs at his bootlaces, smells his armpits, smokes. Once again, he has forgotten to put his empties out on the street at home.

'Do I stink of cheese?', a young woman asks before she hugs her boyfriend who has just boarded the train and the rest of the world around her collapses. 'Embrasse-moi,' she orders him. The request, no, the command is associated in Thaler's mind with the red lips of a former fellow student who had always dragged him along when she went out on the streets, the squares, the boulevards. But Thaler regularly trailed behind on the pavement during the demonstrations, further and further behind, insecure, despondent. Back in his room each time he opened his dormer window, climbed up on a chair and looked out over the city's gables. Towards the sea.

After a friend admonishes him to get himself a rope with a grappling hook so he will have at least a chance to get out of his little attic garret should there ever be a fire, he dreams of a house fire on the following night: he grabs the rope and throws the hook in a wide arc out of the window. The entire rope sails out the dormer window. Thaler's own laughter wakes him and he is freed from his fears for the rest of his stay in Paris.

The truth is, he is nothing but a bother. It's a good thing he left home so spontaneously. The children will have more fun without him, his wife has an easier time of it and has more pluck when he's not there. He just needs a bit of fresh air, that's all.

Three crows chase a buzzard over the beet field his train is crossing. Everything the old woman on the seat across from him sees and hears reminds her of something: of the church bells in her childhood, but softer; of her mother's shoes, but with eyelets and more yellow; of her daughter's son, but taller. One day in September, 1953, more precisely, on the 23rd. 'The beginning of autumn,' her husband says. 'No,' she says, 'back then, autumn began on the 21st. As did spring, by the way.'

On entering, the conductor does not disturb the tightly interlaced couple in the other compartment and looks up the first date of autumn for the elderly man and his wife in the railway timetable. A farmer waits patiently on his tractor at the railway gate. He is wearing a pair of sound absorbers. With his foaming liquid-manure tanker behind him, he seems immune to every one of the world's challenges.

Coloured laundry, forty degrees, gentle cycle, that's how you can spare yourself tiresome ironing, Thaler knows the tricks. A young woman hangs her washing up in her front yard. She has blond hair and brown arms. Thaler would like to bite into her firm flesh. He puts the lemon and honey back into his knapsack. A child throws a ball to the woman, wants to play with her. She lifts the child up and together they wave at the passing train until the last carriage disappears from their sight behind the next range of hills.

Thaler will find his way to the hut even without a map. After he has passed the wayside cross behind the last mountain cabin, it's two hours uphill, following the red-and-white markers until the Krog Pass hut, 1,900 metres above sea level.

The saddle pass always reminds Thaler of the Lapponian Gate high above Abisko. The train had stopped on the open stretch towards Kiruna and the passengers had crossed the northern polar circle on foot. A feeling of unexpected friendship rose among the passengers. And as Thaler made his way alone through the mountains, the bare cliffs to the north resembled a slowly and endlessly flowing river, which seemed to be carrying him.

*On the day she was transferred, the patient was cheered by the short trip through the familiar park and the change to a bed without an automatic elevating mechanism. In any case, she raised her hand noticeably when the nurse left her new room. This gesture was clearly meant to express agreement.*

On the right side of the net, Thaler soared up off the court floor each time, hung for a moment in the air waiting for the set up and spiked the ball over the net between the defenders so they didn't know what hit them. Thaler has the impression later that he never had more success than on the volleyball court. In the showers during this 'year without gravity', he joins in the boisterous water fights and soap games after the matches and sang along with his teammates:

> hoppledehop, two nuts in my sack
> hoppledehoi, two kernels
> when you got a redhead in your shack
> you won't be needing a lantern.

The freshly scrubbed ladies' team always joins the players for a nightcap, they turn their flushed faces towards each other. One night after a victorious match, Thaler conceives his first child with one of the women. And becomes her husband. The couple burrows like hedgehogs in the sudden intimacy, nakedness and approaching parenthood. The unfaltering confidence of Thaler's young wife spreads to him. For a while.

Forty gone. Thaler is now three years older than his father ever was. Not to mention his brother. His two children now come up to just below his shoulders. On lighthearted days, they lift him in the air as if he were made of paper. Sometimes he wishes his children would grow up inside his ribcage—and make it expand.

Arrival in Krogtal. The stationmaster greets the passengers. Thaler returns the greeting. Friendliness always makes him feel slightly embarrassed even though all he wants is to be friendly.

He climbs uphill at a quick pace. The sun is at a slant above him. A late butterfly feigns an appearance of summer. Thaler cannot think when he walks, which is why he is so fond of walking. He keeps his eyes on his shoes, on the path in front of his feet, on the grass along the edges of the path. He avoids the rivulets and feels the first drops of sweat trickle down his back.

A wind rises. A power glider circles over the Krogpass in wide arcs. Thaler stops, looks up: maybe there are two of them in the cockpit. The thought is a momentary stab in his heart.

In front of Thaler's eyes, the path and footbridge seem to be moving on their way, the air shimmers, the ground beneath his feet begins to sway, sweat gushes from every pore. He sits down on a rock, reaches for the honey and sticks his finger deep into the jar.

Wouldn't it be better if he returned home, sent out a new application, caressed his children, worked on his marriage, ate omelettes, ordered Mother's gravestone?

He walks over to the mountain stream, kneels between the rocks and scoops up water with his hands, drinks.

In one of their last sessions of couple's therapy, which his wife had suggested on friends' advice, all he could do was count the buttons on the therapist's high-necked blouse over and over again. At the end of the hour, he had still not come up with definite results.

'Civil twilight,' Thaler says as they step out of the therapist's office into the early evening. An amateur astronomer had explained the concept to him during his military service. It is Thaler's favourite time of day.

Anyone who thinks something of himself finds his way to the professionally led encounter group in the Reformed Church parish hall. Friends and acquaintances of Thaler's gather from every corner of the map. He knows them all, but has forgotten their names.

The course's morning session is filled with preparatory exercises. Exercises for the breath and the pelvic floor. Bits of the Feldenkrais Method are used too. The afternoon session includes copulation training. The condoms are flowery plastic bags, partners alternate. And all the participants join in the experiment with scholarly enthusiasm except for Thaler who had fought against the procedure tooth and nail until he finally awoke.

The highest degree of reality he had ever experienced in his life was still the existence of their children, his only counterevidence to all the rest of the figments and fears, Thaler offers as a coda to the account of his dream over breakfast. His wife considers this, nods, and lays her hand on his forearm which he carefully withdraws.

Thaler returns without having made any progress from a multi-week stay in London during the summer holidays where he had gone in the hope of qualifying to teach English as a subsidiary subject. The city had repelled him, he explains, and on top of that, he suddenly found he could only speak their universal language with distaste.

'Mind the gap!' What's more, even in broad daylight, oil-smeared foxes ran through the underground tunnels in search of food. Completely indifferent, the animals did not take the slightest notice of the clusters of people on the platforms.—And in Thaler's street at midday, men from the banking district sit against the walls in a pub. They hand a pint glass down the line and drop two or three pound coins in the glass when they are happy with the performance of the women dancing on a small platform in the middle of the pub. Then the third woman grabs the metal pole that rises straight up into the bar's heavens one more time with both hands and spreads her thighs so the silver piercing through her inner labia flashes one last time and gives the businessmen courage to return to their jobs behind security locks and bulletproof glass until evening.

After the men have left, Thaler watches the dancers through the pub window as they head home. They're wearing sneakers and carrying shopping bags and joking with one another. Thaler orders another beer and sits at the bar until evening.

'You can expect snow,' the caretaker of the mountain hut says when he meets Thaler on his way down to the valley with his dog. Thaler stands against the sun. He advises Thaler not to try to reach the pass today, tells him where to find the key up there, and asks him to carefully lock the hut up in the morning and to put out the fire. Thaler nods, from now on he will be entirely alone. His strength returns.

Thaler continues uphill, his long steps set the suspension bridge swinging ominously.

The ridges in the cliff on the opposite side of the valley draw closer together as if they were petrified during a slow escape.

Two hours later he reaches the hut. Clouds drift over the saddle, the sun slips towards the horizon like a bright coin. The grey wolf will carry it across the underside of the globe overnight and up into the new day. That is how the Laplanders imagine it.

Thaler watches the Alpine choughs' wild acrobatics above the chimney, sees their open yellow beaks. Did the birds accompany him up here or where they already here—should he weep? With joy?

Until recently it was still common on the other side of the valley to lay out the dead in the living room for three days before accompanying them on their last march, Thaler had read somewhere. The living room with the corpse was a place of silent mourning. The kitchen, on the other hand, was a place for sympathy and conversation and a glass of wine or schnapps to soothe dry throats.

Because this custom is slowly dying out among younger generations, the village's resident architect had sought a workable solution instead of the usual funeral home and included space in the usual sequence of living room, hallway, kitchen. On the ground floor of the small, two-storey house that was built below the village church, there is now a public room for the dead to lie in repose. On the upper floor, there is a large kitchen where mourners can sit together and talk, eat and drink.

Thaler was never able to properly say goodbye to his dead, they were always put in a coffin right away and shoved in a morgue. He wants to go see the funeral home after he has crossed the mountain.

*In the hospital garden, children were playing in the sand between the flower beds, the first drops spattered on the asphalt. White steam billowed from the doors of the laundry. The newspaper displays on the kiosk recounted, in black and white and in colour, the lives of those photographed. I stood indecisively under the awning, leafed through the magazines, looked at the pictures, read the captions until the saleswoman asked me what I would like. I bought cigarettes and a bar of dark chocolate and sat under the new building's awning next to a new mother whose slippers reminded me of a pair of swans. I let the chocolate slowly melt in my mouth and took drags on a cigarette. A flash of lighting hit the weeping willow with a loud crack and split the tree. The young mother fled into the tall house in terror. A grey heron landed on the edge of the biotope.*

The stove is still warm, Thaler fans the flames and sets water from the nearby creek to boil in a pot filled with peppermint tea. He sees the hunting knife hanging on the doorframe—a film of rust coats the long blade—and he counts the light points of the deer antler over the chimney; there are twelve. A spider has spun its web between the two beams of the 'Prize' and is staying hidden while a curious dormouse looks down from the top of the cabinet. Outside the first stars appear, their light is friendly but cold.

The fact that he misses absolutely nothing up here shocks Thaler but cheers him up at the same time. He would know the names of two constellations—Orion and the Big Dipper. But he doesn't look for them. A jet crosses the sky, he would not like to be sitting with the passengers. He locks the door of the hut, wraps himself in the blanket and stretches out on the bench next to the stove. He chases a ghostly pair of children from the dark room and falls asleep immediately.

No animals. No dream. No longing. He lies there like a piece of summer furniture that has been stacked in the corner. At three in the morning he wakes and chips water off the thick snowdrift outside. He dips his sleepy face in the flakes.

Feldspar, quartz and mica, the three minerals gleam from Thaler's left wrist, like a delicate tattoo under his skin. They are the finest particles of rock, fine particles of dust only found in the area around the Seffinen-furgge Pass. As a result of a minor fall during a required hike at high altitude with his class in second-ary school, the mountain quite literally got under his skin.

All the while, on clear days, the crown of the Alps had trumpeted, threatened, had been enthroned in his ears and behind his back since his earliest childhood. 'We go up the mountains through morning dew, fallera ...' Barefoot. Uphill and down. As happy and healthy as Peter the goatherd. And when the Alps grew bright with splendour, the free Swiss prayed, as they'd had to sing starting in the fifth grade as soon as they set foot in the foothills of the Alps, and it gave Thaler a fever every time.

On each school trip he would be suddenly over-come with a feeling of homesickness for the gentle notes and for the green hills of the Swiss plateau. For his brother too. And for pale Klara in Frankfurt and her land flat enough for wheelchairs. He had never had much stomach for the indestructible, invincible, the precipitously looming, the sheer obduracy of the rock faces along with Heidi and Peter the goatherd.

Years later, Thaler travelled to the sea, out into the flat-lands. With sand between the pine and fir trees. And sand between his teeth. He landed on the edge of deserts, he swam in the open sea, stared into jaggedness. Irritated, fascinated and more indulgently attuned to each flap of a fin than the Alpine peaks of his homeland, the mountains became accessible to him only after he had experienced the counter-mountainscape of the watery deep—the cliffs rise on the beach, hard, soft and mutable. The sand on his skin resembles the sand under his skin. And so the cliffs are also destructible, in the end, drifting sand like Klara, like his brother, as he is himself too.

Thaler reaches for the cold tea on the table, sucks on a lemon, licks honey out of the jar and carefully folds up the wool blanket and puts it back on the pile. By candlelight, he writes an entry in the hut's logbook. 'I am here. I don't know any more than that. There is nothing more I can do. (Kafka, *The Hunter Gracchus*). Thank you for the right to hospitality. Greetings, Peter Thaler,' he writes in his almost indecipherable hand on a new page.—His own name seems so strange to him, his handwriting completely unfamiliar. Although he is not Catholic, he sprinkles a little holy water around the hut with the fir twig in the tray next to the ceramic bowl, closes the door and puts the key on the splitting block behind the store of firewood. He sets off in the direction of the pass. It is still deepest night.

The depth of the snow increases steadily. Thaler's eyes are burning, but he does not think of turning back. He keeps on with a fierce expression, relishes the workings of his body, his sure footing. His legs are cold and wet up to and past his knees, his raincoat, which the wind roughly penetrates, is stiff and thin, Thaler doesn't fight it.

Up on the pass, the storm rages, a billowing white sail flies directly at him over the crest. Thaler leans into the wind and it tears his peaked cap from his head, he snatches at it, loses his foothold, slips, falls. He slides feet first down an escarpment, tries to brake by flailing his arms and legs, his legs and forehead are beaten raw against the rock face, his foot is broken. Thaler heard the bone break. He comes to rest lying on his back in the snow in a gentle hollow, dazed with pain—and with a strange sense of satisfaction in mind:

Something like this had always been foreseen for him, he has to believe. His life to date has been nothing but deferral, delay, skirmishes. Now it is serious. Finally.

Thaler is startled by a foolish memory from his distant past, he sees himself reaching for a silver-coloured whipped-cream dispenser and, at the same time, he looks around the white valley basin—to the roaring laughter of his colleagues, he fills some grinning blowhard's mouth and throat with white cream. The young man waves his arms in distress, turns red in the face, nearly chokes.—But only now is Thaler appalled at his unthinking pitilessness and hardness. Let it go, let it go right now, he thinks and starts to breathe calmly. He talks to his victim, talks to himself and another wave of dizziness washes over him.

Most of all, he'd like to be barefoot. His clammy fingers fumble with the wet shoe on his hot foot. He gives up and in the same moment concedes that by 'let it go', he also means 'get going'. Beginning. Fresh start. The fingers of his right hand twitch out SOS in Morse code. Three dots, three dashes, three dots.

Thaler works his body into an upright position, spits in the snow, examines himself, listens attentively to the darkness around him. It's dead quiet. He lets himself sink back into his hollow. He feels so miserable and forlorn.

Here and there narrow strips of the sky clear. Thaler looks up at the gaps in the clouds, a satellite crosses the firmament and creates fleeting new constellations with the stars, for a second a milk-white city lights up in the depths of space, enormous, white animals drift over the ridges, the silhouette of a girl: 'The Star Talers!', Thaler thinks involuntarily and pictures himself as the naked, shivering orphan in the fairy tale, the way he had felt at the celebration with the sparkles and volcanic shower of stars—or imagines the warm crater of a volcano opening up under his backside, surrounding and engulfing him, as the volcano had swallowed Empedocles. Then the light in the sky goes out again.

Sometimes Thaler is not at all sure if what he is experiencing is real or not. He grabs at his leg, laughs incredulously and calls his own name 'Thaler!' with all his strength into the white-speckled dawn. No echo returns. Instead, the valley is filled with a roaring like the one that used to fill the turbine halls of the Brown Boveri Company. Cranes driving up, hoisting chains rattling—Thaler was allowed to visit his father between the lathes and the flashing rotors, his father lifted and held him protectively. It was the first time Thaler could remember feeling utterly lost. And the first time he saw his father standing lost and forlorn in the immense halls.

Thaler must have nodded off. Rows of seats rose steeply around him. He dreamt of a sad clown, reached for the red nose, brushed it away and was awake. Hunger and thirst afflict him. He eats snow.

'Help is coming from Bregenz,' Thaler had read in Kafka. The sentence remained in his mind, enigmatically isolated. He believes more deeply in Kafka's prose than he does in the dear Lord, but at the moment he would prefer not to share that with the Almighty. Help is coming from Bregenz. Thaler imagines God the Father as a Voralberger, complete with hat, and is happy he can appeal to Him for help in his own blessed dialect: *Hilf mir, bitte, hilf mir*!

The snow has stopped, it is dawning. And despair finally sets in earnest. A storm of choughs descends on Thaler. He tries to slide downhill, but the terrain refuses to cough him up.

The snow gradually covers Thaler in a soft, white blanket, cools his forehead and eyelids, alleviates the cold in the rest of his body and clears the blind spot in his eyeball, his speechless lips, the dark silhouette of the two children he left behind, everything that had always driven him out into this thin air. The search for solid ground beneath his feet, stores of rock for the winter, an anchoring in the landscape and pictures, in the light.

Recently, his attention was drawn to the two scars on his neck; as an infant, he had been given up for dead, the two incisions were made quite late. For an instant, Thaler imagines he sees outlines of his devastated, young parents behind the glass in the hospital ward, then, behind the glass of the coffin—he can distinctly recall—his brother's face. Time, his time is now contracting into the two indentations on his neck, palpably, and in the picture of his two children. With the course of their lives, their astonishment, doubt and laughter before the world. The scars hurt.

When you leave home on a trip and keep going, you will one day return to your own doorstep, according to a pilgrim's report from the Middle Ages. Years earlier, Thaler had noticed this sentence and never forgotten it. Thaler gathers all his strength, shouts: 'Rise up and walk!'—Jesus never made any real jokes, at least none were handed down, the thought suddenly strikes Thaler. And why weren't anecdotes about him passed on? Thaler groans: True love of one's fellow man and fidelity to all divinities and founders of religions should not rest upon their wounds, wonders and commandments, but should also be measured against their sense of humour, for God's sake!

'Rise up and walk!' However, he must have a few broken ribs as well if that short adjuration caused him such terrible pain even when he simply drew breath.

He won't be missed at home until evening, the children will ask where he is and stay sitting at the table, in silence. Or they will hole themselves up in their rooms and shove a disc roughly into the slot, and shoot the stick figures on the screen.

Lena will put a candle on the living-room table and will place the flat of her hands over her nose and mouth like a gable and will breathe warm air into her cold palms. She might call up a friend and together they will decide, angry and discouraged at Thaler's absence and silence, to do something about it tomorrow and to see about things then.

Around two o'clock in the morning, after the children have finally stopped making noise, sleep will finally overpower Lena, or maybe fear for Thaler will get the upper hand.—Good Lord, Thaler moans through clenched teeth, good Lord, Lena! Nothing more occurs to him.

In despair. Lost. And withdrawn. Thaler's condition changes rapidly and each new state is grounded in the last: despair in pretension, withdrawal in the sense of being lost.

Thaler calls out, sniffs the air, listens, rubs his cold torso, calms down again. On the mountain face across from him, over which springtime is slowly creeping, a small slab of snow breaks off and flies down into the valley. Then the sky clears completely and the sun sets its sights on him, thaws him out. Thaler spreads out his red rain gear. As a signal. He closes his eyes, projects a movie on his sun-drenched inner eyelids, sees himself at the seaside with his children, they bury him until only his head is sticking out of the sand—then Thaler conjures up an aeroplane in his thoughts.

He hears the engine coming from far off, it's a Bücker two-seater with a radial engine flying behind his swollen lids instead of the air-rescue service flying into the valley basin. It turns upside down and after a careful loop, it flies off quickly. Thaler can't wave the stunt pilot down to him.

Snow has fallen
Long before its time,
They are pelting me with snowballs,
My path is blocked with snow.

Thaler composes a letter in his head: Dear children, he writes. Dearest.

My house, it has no gables
It has grown so old,
The bolts have all been broken
My room is very cold.

His letter follows an ancient melody he hums to himself, because he can't come up with words of his own, he sings softly and sweetly the last verse as well.

Oh, my dear, show me mercy
For I am so very wretched
And clasp me in your arms,
That's how winter will end.

That is how winter will end, Thaler repeats and slumps, exhausted, onto his side.

*When the rain let up, instead of getting in the car and returning home, I strolled across the slippery lawn and returned to the tract of old buildings and went into the sick room one more time. Again, I paused in the doorway, another man stood in the room. He bound up my mother's jaw, offered his condolences and handed me a yellow chrysanthemum to place between her folded hands.*

*So, that is what the end looks like, only slightly different from the long wait for recovery that preceded it. Maybe the air was drier in the room and tickled my skin like sand. If the nurse hadn't been standing there, I would have laughed out loud again.——In trousers that were too short, I stand politely at the edge of the school garden with a bent sunflower in my hand. The black-and-white photograph was hung on Mother's kitchen cabinet for years.*

*The sun had emerged from behind the drifting clouds and now shone mercilessly in the dead woman's room. I wiped the sweat from my brow. And I went home.*

A sharp wind rises before the sun sinks again between the towering cliffs and takes with it the last vague hope of rescue. After waking with a start, Thaler howls like a wounded animal. He stares, no, marvels at the blue gloaming that follows on the heels of the light's descent, and is again wide awake. He pulls his rain jacket tighter around him and is ready to freeze to death.

He looks stoically up through his observation slit at the rapidly darkening sky. The night will be a clear one, that he knows.—Venus appears. Should he speak to the star, and how many wishes does he have left, what would he command a shooting star, if one passed over him?

He thinks of his children. And of the old Swiss Confederacy, of all things, the Battle of Sempach, the man who steps out on stage and says: Take care of my wife and children! But Thaler doesn't want to create an entrance for anyone any more, he doesn't want to win a war, just peace, if possible.

'Last year's honey harvest was a good one: perhaps this one sentence is the only one we should leave behind for our descendants. In honour of the bees,' is the last entry Thaler's friends will find in his notebook at home.

No coat of arms, no banner, no real weather. The encounter takes place in a sand-coloured expanse of inhospitableness. It occurs between a fair, gentle knight, no, a lady riding a small grey horse—the saddle is scarlet, as are her shoes—and a black knight on the back of a burly black stallion. The knight wears a helmet and armour. Behind him rides his lord, more sensed than seen. The gravitational pull of the black knight extends stoically ahead of him from the depths.

It is assumed that the painter created the picture in the last year of his life, using a broad brush. The lines typical of his earlier work are nowhere to be seen in this picture, which now appears in the snow before Thaler, almost within reach. The setting is far from Henri de Toulouse Lautrec's *Moulin Rouge*. It lies in a no-man's, in an every-man's land. And the painter is ill, mortally ill, he knows this.

> Death can ride a black or grey horse,
> Death can smile as he dances,
> He beats the drum loud,
> He beats the drum well:
> Everyone, everyone dies perforce.

Yet again, Thaler has a song on his lips, a *danse macabre*, 'grave and ponderous, after a Dance of Death song from the Rhineland, poet and composer unknown', read the footnote in the upper-school songbook. It was one of the few songs that got under even the half-grown boys' skins and had them humming along almost like death itself.—It was that old *danse macabre* melody that had hung in the air the first time Thaler happened on Lautrec's painting. He is surprised and strangely pleased by this echoing reserve for emergencies.

The drum beat, the hooves, the struggle as a fight for survival, as well as the heavy and complicated turns of love that are captured in the painting, febrile, that captivate Thaler, who has experienced all of this like a blow to the chest: this distinct inevitability of one's existence, which over the course of his life had seemed harder and harder to bear without the assistance of pictures and stories.

*Deux chevaliers en armure* is the painting's makeshift title, probably given to it later. The German translation of the title means 'Medieval Battle Scene', but there is not just war in the air, even if the painting shows the hooves under which we will fall, under which Thaler will fall in the coming night. Because the woman rider also exerts a pull, bright and effortless, a kind of counter-dance, so to speak. And her eye does not hold the battle, or horror, but the Grail. Or do the two actually hold each other, knight and rider, in their hearts, souls and minds wherever they go?

Like man and wife?

Like life and death?

Thaler closes his eyes and sees himself as an image in this November.

When Thaler opens his eyes again, he once again sees a soldier sitting on the edge of the path. The soldier is tired, has laid down his weapons, lance and sword. The full moon is reflected in the surface of the pond behind him. Thaler has not forgotten this powerful man since their first and only meeting—Arnold Böcklin's mercenary looks across the valley at his house at night. There is a light in the window, warmth. He is a mere stone's throw from home. But the man cannot manage the last few steps. He will return to battle. Without a word, he will rejoin the ranks of the Swiss Confederates who are inured to death. Until they finally retreat from Marignano, defeated. A parade of ghosts.

Thaler wants to raise the army again, to make two angel wings in the snow as a sign. But his muscles no longer obey him. His entire body is numb and stiff with cold.

No, he feels no fear of death, rather an almost indecent sense of relief that he need not either advance or retreat, dead tired as he is.

He reaches for the few pages he had packed at home and had stuffed under his lower back as insulation, lays them on his chest. Hopefully he has at least recorded Mother's death decorously on paper. The story could have been a new beginning.

*The Argentine*

1

During his worst night on the high seas, Grandfather bit into the picture of the beloved he had left behind in Europe, and this soothed him. On the day he left she stood as if turned to stone near the tracks as he thundered by his parents' house on the early train, letting his handkerchief flutter in the wind. The morning after the stormy night on the deck of the old *Virginia*, he crawled on all fours to the railing. There lay the sea, as if nothing had happened. He vomited once more and breathed deeply.

The crossing on the freighter quickly taught him to let happen whatever would happen: wind, weather, the captain's moods, the stoker's curses, the vice-like stomach cramps on stormy seas. There was a taste of rust in his mouth but he let nothing show. A sailor lost two fingers of his right hand trying to tie up cargo that had broken loose. Three whales followed the ship, three fountains.

When Grandfather landed in Buenos Aires after weeks
on the ocean, the ground rolled under his feet for several days. The sailor with the bad hand was carried
ashore in a fever. Grandfather carried his small inheritance in a cloth bag under his clothes. But Amelie had
become unrecognizable in the photograph. I felt your
bites deep in my heart, every single one, she wrote in
a letter that was never to reach the New World.

In the same envelope, there had also been a new picture
of Amelie, one she had cut from a group photograph
of her Confirmation class since she had none of herself
alone. Because she stood on the edge of the small
group, she did not need to seriously wound any of
them with the straight razor Father had left in the
kitchen. She would have preferred a new picture, but
she was in a hurry to send the letter and a photographer
was expensive. Even so, she had already cut off her
braids for her Confirmation. Besides, her face had not
grown to look much older in the four years since then.
She had carefully verified this in the bathroom mirror
and tinted her lips in the picture light red with a
coloured pencil moistened on her tongue.

Two years later, Grandfather turned his horse around
and returned to Buenos Aires from the pampas. He
sold his saddle, spurs, *bolas* and bridle to a newcomer

from Lower Austria. He wrapped the long knife that was part of every gaucho's gear in newspaper, and brought it home in his luggage. It later disappeared in Grandmother's cutlery drawer. On the front page of the crumpled paper, which the traveller flattened out with the palm of his hand, was a picture of a radiant pair, Juan Domingo Perón, in uniform, and his young wife, Eva. They stood there as if in a film.

We were gathered again for the first time since completing school, twice as old now as we were then. The head pupil already had hair implants. We all remembered the sight of Lena's grandfather well—a quiet man with a hat, who walked in a leisurely pace up and down the school courtyard during the long recesses while the classrooms were being aired. Now and then he kicked a stray ball back to his older students, separated two heated roughnecks, helped a heavy student onto the high bar or, when necessary, had a serious word before rejoining his two waiting colleagues from the middle and lower levels. Together they continued their walk. Grandfather had been buried the week before, Lena told us. He was the first person close to her to have died; we were still young.

2

Not long after the Second World War, and as soon as he had completed his primary-school-teaching certificate and his subsequent military training at one of the bases of the steadfast Swiss army, Grandfather steamed off to South America from Southampton to become a gaucho—to get away from the Old World that had run aground—in search of a new, more humane corner of the earth. Riding himself raw on his own saddle appealed to him far more as a way of life, Lena explained, than his professors' worn trouser seats, though he remained a passionate reader to the end.

The young man had already swallowed, like gulps of fresh air, accounts of Fridtjof Nansen who skied across Greenland, drifted through the Arctic Sea for three years on the 'Fram,' and finally was awarded the Nobel Prize for his work as a League of Nations high commissioner. He had also devoured accounts of Roald Admundsen's daring adventures, although Admundsen, who had subdued the Antarctic night and won the race with Robert Falcon Scott to the South Pole, had never appealed to him much. Scott's journals of struggling and dying in the eternal snow, on the other hand, pierced him straight to the marrow, like red-hot iron. And Joseph Conrad's *Heart of Darkness* accompanied him into his own shadow realm. But Grandfather was also very taken with the ideas and adventures of Johann Heinrich Pestalozzi along with his unparalleled dedication to teaching orphans in Stans, and, later, to founding a school.

Back in Switzerland, Grandfather decided to devote the long remainder of his working years to the small village school. Presumably his longing for Amelie, which had re-awoken over time, had grown too strong to resist. Or maybe it was the homesickness that people like to claim eventually overcomes all Swiss who live in distant lands.

Once, Grandfather came upon a village of Swiss-Argentinians outside of Santa Fe. They welcomed him like a messiah, because the settlers quickly determined that he too had Oberwallish roots. '*Chumm inna!*' they said. But he never could have stayed there. He found their village life much too narrow. Lena paused in her story and looked intently into our faces for a moment, as if she were searching for traces of gold.

3

Back then in Argentina, Grandfather had once explained, he became a halfway decent tango dancer instead of a real gaucho only because of a stubborn bout of hay fever. His inner cowhand no doubt gave in too easily to his allergy to a certain grass. This new career training, if you can call it that, was in turn only possible because, almost like a sleepwalker, he kept delaying his return home. His hay fever probably could have been cured but the tango cannot be treated medically.

Where did everyone end up after leaving school, Lena asked in the same breath of me and a few classmates who had come up to us after the official welcome, some of whom had travelled here over great distances. Nicely dressed, we stood together in a circle. Australia was mentioned as a location, as were Paris, London, New York and South Africa. The Caribbean was not left out as a vacation spot. However, many from our primary-school class had simply stayed in the area, alone or in various relationships. Two showed us pictures of their children. The oldest of these children was already ten years old, the youngest only two months. New groups of shared interests were forming.

Lena and I remained standing together next to the closed piano. On the soccer field adjacent to the hotel garden, a game was in progress. Through the large plate glass window, we watched the players running around in their red and green jerseys and the small group of feverishly enthusiastic spectators. Exactly as they had twenty years before, players were constantly getting hurt. The referee held up a yellow card and a medic—it was actually still the indestructible Lehmann —ran across the field with his blue pail of water to press a cold, wet sponge to the fouled player's injury. The aides, at the ready with stretcher in hand, never got their chance to step in since the game was quickly resumed.

I asked Lena to tell me more about her grandfather. I had hardly known my grandparents. They were only occasionally mentioned in fairy tales and the wolf always ate them. We found a small round table set for four and sat down. After the meal, we were meant to 'rotate' so that everyone would have a chance to speak with everyone else. Patrick, the evening's organizer, had thought this up. On our left hung a colourful aerial view of the renovated country hotel, although there was no trace of the adjacent football field. There were three tulips from Amsterdam on each table. Ours were white.

4

'Yes, yes, the work of the dance' is all Grandfather would answer and then nothing more whenever anyone tried to find out about his career as a dancer in the New World. His reputation as a tango virtuoso stubbornly stuck to the soles of his shoes on his return and was not to be shaken off. Although Grandfather soon showed himself to be one of the most half-hearted dancers on the local dance floor and he never made any effort to prove himself otherwise, the myth of the great dancer stuck to him.

Even his beautiful, vivacious wife who, early in their marriage, would have been only too happy to talk him into an English waltz or the Charleston, still quietly believed the myth for years.

After five years of moving from one temporary job or substitute position to another throughout the Swiss Prealps, Amelie and he settled with their small family in the small village on the lake. They gradually built a small refuge with a large vegetable and flower garden and even a few animals came and went. After their last move, they slept in separate rooms so that the night could bend over them undisturbed, Amelie explained, and they could meet again the next morning with a fresh embrace, as if returning to their breakfast table from distant lands.

Still, Grandfather had no desire to lead an active communal life in this particular spot, as befit a proper schoolteacher. The school was community enough for him, he said. He even avoided serving with the volunteer fire department on the grounds that he did not want to encourage his students to arson, since they would be missing lessons whenever their teacher had to be away extinguishing a fire. He did not offer his assistance as director or lead dancer to any of the local choirs, music groups or traditional costume dance groups.

'I have danced myself out,' he is meant to have stoically responded as he looked off into the distance, according to one of the area's most insightful group leaders, who had tried once again to enlist him as head of a folk-dance organization. The Argentine, as he was called, not without respect, even forcefully declined requests for temporary assistance. He only led the closing conga line at the end of every school year, with a wheezing accordion at his chest.

Like the Pied Piper of Hamelin, Grandfather led the children in a long arc out of the gymnasium decorated with paper garlands into the fresh air. His route led them through gorse and hazel bushes and climbing poles to the paved playground and over the deep sand landing pit, arid grassland and a small stream, ending up at the old cemetery wall. The Argentine scaled it in one bold leap so that the children, with bright and sweaty faces, could pass before him, in two rows, singing and laughing. Behind him lay the dead.

5

Many of the men and women in the village had passed through the Argentine's school. Workshops and factories, important political duties, and honorary offices lay in their hands. Usually the responsibility passed from father to son, though with time daughters were not exempt when it came time for the boldest of the students to ask the Argentine, at the beginning of every school year at some point during the geography lesson that critical question: 'Where is Argentina?'

'I will explain that to you later,' Grandfather always answered calmly and let the class giggle. The choreography of his closing conga line could be considered an answer to the question of Argentina's geographical location, had any one looked for an answer on that map.

'I play both sides out of sheer joy and who would hold that against me?' he countered those critical voices who considered his daring course along the cemetery wall quite simply blasphemous. 'God is not dead—we certainly hope he isn't.' The Anabaptists and other orthodox Christians in the district could hardly object to this answer either. And because everyone considered the Argentine a good teacher, over time they let him indulge his quirks without protest and also put fewer obstacles in the way of his new public library.

Whales sing, bees dance, birds and monkeys communicate through signals. The critical difference between our means of expression and theirs lies in our ability to express the real as well as the unreal. The future, the conditional, as well as lies and expressions of hope and of longing, plans and suppositions, memory and imagination, they are all at our disposal. 'Utopias, quite simply, exist in books,' Grandfather explained in his written justification to the local authorities for the founding of a public library. '—When reading, we go on journeys, undergo adventures, think ourselves evermore deeply into other modes of living and delve evermore deeply into our own lives as well.'

He called the small reading room behind the library *Pascal's Room*, and he often withdrew there for hours at a time. He read new publications and always returned to *Don Quixote*. In his desk drawer he also kept a copy in Spanish of the great novel, over which he sometimes murmured to himself softly, to have a bit of Spanish music in his ears and to keep from losing the language completely. He had originally called his room *Patagonia*. Only later did he christen it *Pascal's Room*. And that is what it remained. Sometimes he also just sat there quietly and gazed at the wall in front of him.

6

Lena blew the bangs of her short hair off her forehead. The appetizer had just been served, shrimp cocktail on a bed of avocado. The alumni had divided themselves into groups for conversation and none of our former classmates had rejoined us. Only one table was unoccupied, yet no one knew the whereabouts of those missing. We did not speak. And since I made no attempt to engage in the kind of entertainment that was surging towards us ever-more animatedly from nearby tables, Lena took up where she had left off.

She herself was in part to thank, Lena said, laughing, that the distant love that finally drew Grandfather back from South America to the European continent eventually grew into a close and lasting one. There is a picture of her as a small girl in which she looks just like her grandfather. Her mother wrote *The little grandfather* next to it in the photo album. Because of tragic circumstances, however, her grandparents only ever had a one-child family. Her mother's younger brother drowned in the icy waters of the nearby lake soon after his fifth birthday. And a 'replacement' for Pascal was simply unthinkable for both of them.

'Even now, I could scream,' Lena's grandmother would say occasionally but would immediately take herself in hand, calmly holding her wrists that had began to ache very early. And abruptly, she would begin to talk about the flight of the homing pigeons who faithfully delivered the neighbours' greetings every morning. Their flight resembled a giant horizontal figure eight.

The pigeon trainer confessed to her once that every time he travelled to the city, he would take along a basket of homing pigeons and release them there. Those who did not find their way home automatically became city pigeons. That way he controlled his stock of reliable messengers.

Or Grandmother would retell the story of the dormice who appeared every day. At the time, they were renting a small house, a lopsided hut with leaking eaves. The cat chased the mice and Grandmother went after the dormice, until one day she simply branded the captured animals with red nail polish to prove to her kind-hearted husband that the cursed critters were already back in the house by the time he returned with his empty traps after granting them amnesty in the nearby forest. 'You can't imagine people more simultaneously composed and fanciful,' Lena said, 'even if Grand-father had become a bit strange over the years.'

He would get worked up over the lack of care that he saw spreading rapidly through almost all areas of life. 'Ruthlessness and material greed. A wasteland, a spiritual wasteland, wherever one looks, combined with an inhuman indifference and a supposedly global outlook, which is characterized primarily by the view that everything can be bought from anywhere and sold everywhere.' He would say this and wipe these serious reproaches from the table with an agitated movement of his hand. Then he would ask about the position of the sun, about family, about our friends and personal matters.——But in private, he never insisted, Lena's mother said once again at his funeral. It was not in reproach but in praise. As a single mother and so-called free woman, she was particularly grateful to the teacher for this.

## 7

I felt an odd sense of remove while listening to the account of this unusual life, but I also remembered that someone had recently reproached me for revealing very little about myself in conversation, and so I preemptively offered my required share. I told Lena that I gave up theology after getting my degree and was now searching for a new or related field of interest. For the time being, I was living quite well from occasional assignments as conference coordinator and panel moderator and from editing short essays in my own and in related fields of study.

'Everyone is holding conferences these days,' Lena said.

'Stock in ethics conferences is running especially high,' I replied. 'Conferences focused on what they call questions of values. Perhaps that, in itself, is an alarming sign—an official notice of loss of fundamental concepts of value. You're there to offer your two cents and then are questioned by the former chairman of the board of a major bank, widely considered the branch's chief con man.'

'Not even the old philosopher and poet Matthias Claudius is spared attacks any more,' Lena answered and blew her nose in a tissue.

She had followed her love of the visual arts and worked as a curator of a respected private collection, for which she was, at the moment, preparing a catalogue presenting Jean-Siméon Chardin and Giorgio Morandi as brothers in spirit across two centuries. One of its main themes would be to examine their kinship through the ways they related to objects. Marcel Proust, after all, had learnt from Chardin that a pear is as alive as a woman.

Lena had recently returned to working with old-master paintings, which she prefers because it's easier to differentiate mere semblance from the real thing in the old masters than in the works of many contemporary artists—and to distinguish essence from attitude, art from the latest trends. And from business.

But we turned back to the Argentine as if we felt we hadn't yet lived enough, hadn't heard or seen enough to actually need to talk about these things.—The cheerful din from the neighbouring tables indicated that the time for telling anecdotes from our shared school years had come and colourful jokes would not be far behind. And Lena didn't pick up the thread of our conversation without first recalling the scrawny substitute we'd startled one day while the classroom was being aired by throwing a wet snowball at the blackboard right next to his head. Holding a short piece of chalk and with his tongue between his ruined teeth, he had been immersed in his calligraphy. Feigning outrage, we all ran to the open window to look for the villain in the snow, but he, of course, was long gone. Lacking a handkerchief, Staubacher wiped himself and his glasses dry with the rag for cleaning the blackboard, after which he looked like a miner from a chalk pit.

Grandfather was right-handed. He had given his last slap in 1968, halfway through his teaching years. And he gave it with his left hand. An older student had ruined an apple tree in the schoolyard and Grandfather's hand was itching. And because the boy quickly covered his left cheek, Grandfather hauled off with his left, hard enough to hurt. Back in the classroom he realized that his Confirmation watch had not withstood the blow and was stopped at the very time he had lost control. A mix of shame and an urge to chuckle washed over him. He took off the watch and hung it next to the mirror on the inside of his closet door as a reminder.

For Christmas, Amelie gave him a semi-automatic watch with a window for the date and a red second hand. The time of sporadic blows was over.

8

Grandfather lay in his coffin very gently, almost smiling. They said goodbye to him in the foyer in front of the big oven. When they were done, a young woman closed the small window for the coffin and let him be drawn slowly into the blaze. Mother had given everyone in the family a chafing candle and sent round a lighter. 'We are stokers and coal in one,' said Lena thoughtfully. 'But the place was light and clean and the room was as comfortably warm as a bakery.'

So here it ends, she must have thought involuntarily, but without real fear, as she studied the switches and levers of the incinerator. After a time, the young woman withdrew with a silent nod into a glass-fronted cabinet to complete the cremation procedure in peace.

As everyone gathered on Lena's mother's signal out in the square in front of the crematorium before making their way across to the chapel where they could officially take their leave of the deceased and accept the first condolences from friends and relatives, a powerful gust of wind blew from a cloudless sky through the crowns of the trees in the nearby cemetery.—Everyone would have liked to believe the roaring of the wind was a sign from the dead man, that he had been able to take leave of this earth.

*Maybe something will come of us. Once. By chance. For ever* was written in feathery script as some kind of wish on the wall behind the altar table. New building techniques replacing the massive old archangel. The light fell on a smooth glass console, on which was carved the letters' mirror image so that their shadow is reflected onto the light-coloured plaster underneath. This discreet portent, Lena remarked, seamlessly fit the account of Grandfather's life her mother had given in a steady voice.

Following the wishes of the deceased, after the funeral service ended, almost all the mourners filed over, in a long column somewhat reminiscent of a conga line, to the nearby restaurant for a light meal. It was not long before everyone had eaten and laughter was not in short supply. At this point the groups of our former classmates, most of them grey, gathered to sing one more time, as an end to the evening, Grandfather's favourite song, a lovely sad melody that every grade had had to hear.

KLAUS MERZ

*S'isch äben e Mönsch of Ärde,*
*Won I möcht bi-n-ihm sy.*

(*There is someone in the world*
*by whose side I'd like to be.*)

Grandfather had only gradually grown close to his
wife: first across the Atlantic, then over their young
son's grave.—Amelie had initially had to let the man
she loved follow his childhood dream into the
unknown. She'd sensed this was the only way she could
win his love, and maybe not even then, but from the
very first moment, she was utterly under his spell.—If
Grandfather had perceived Amelie's readiness early on,
he would probably have been frightened to death.
Instead, he rode out into the Argentinian pampas without once looking back.

9

Amelie helped with the housework or ran the shop
when her mother worked in the garden or took in work
knotting new camouflage nets for the Swiss army. Ten
years earlier, Amelie's father had left, full of passion
and fire, and was killed soon after in the Spanish Civil
War. His desertion from the small, hedgehog-like

country cost their shop almost all of its customers, until the death notice arrived and the customers returned, feeling they could shop there again out of pity.

The community representative laid the official document on the sales counter and offered the council's condolences. If her father had returned from the war alive, he would have been thrown in jail as a mercenary for a foreign military service and their imported goods store would have folded.

Amelie often stood, waiting for customers and thought of her two 'legionnaires', her father and her beloved, in sadness, in love and in anger.

The main course had been cleared and the cooking praised. 'Imported goods,' Lena said as steak from Argentina was written on the menu.

Amelie had inherited her stubborn heart from her father. She did not want to win a battle, but the war, even if she would not have expressed herself in military terms. She had an aura of something at once pure and unyielding. Even in old age, her eyes were dark blue. When Grandfather's steamer from South America docked in Southampton, Amelie stood on the pier. She had scrimped to save up the travel fare.

Together, the young couple slowly returned home to Switzerland across a Europe waking from a nightmare.—His father, in contrast to Amelie's, had never, in his entire life, crossed the border of his own country, the Argentine told the woman he held dear. But in Lausanne, the farthest his father had ever travelled, he had met his beloved in a public park on a Sunday afternoon, and they became engaged there in the stillness.

As the sun sank behind the Jura that evening, the betrothed pair had to return to the masters by whom each was employed: the bride as kitchen help in a merchant's household—lamps, furnishings, tapestries—and Grandfather's father to his miller in Langenthal.

However, before he reported in to work early on the Monday morning, Grandfather's father let the paternoster carry him up and down the mill's four floors and mezzanines as he sang. He married his young bride within the year. Twenty years together remained to them.

Towards the end of his years in primary school, Grandfather found in the attic of his parents' house his father's dusty, handmade crystal radio receiver, long thought lost. This is the simplest kind of receiver for amplitude-modulated high-frequency signals, he had explained to Amelie. Built exactly as he had seen it described in the Pestalozzi almanac under 'handicraft instructions,' consisting of a tuned circuit coupled to an antenna and a semiconductor crystal detector to extract the audio signal. It was a tuned radio-frequency receiver with limited receptivity and selectivity. Headphones also lay next to it. The dust was easily blown from the appliance so that after only a brief search, he was actually able to hear whispers of distant worlds in the headphones. More mysterious and wondrous than the mundane Bakelite radio near the credenza.— This was probably the original source of his later wanderlust.

Grandfather always claimed that there was no finer finale, Lena recounted, than the one in 1924, the year of his birth. Switzerland versus Uruguay. Grandfather's father had promised his neighbours, as owner of this handmade crystal receiver, that he would broadcast the Olympic finals with amplifiers and loudspeakers out into the square of their housing development. Tables were set up outside. A full hour before the starting whistle, all the chairs were taken and crates of beer set out. However, there was only a hissing in the air and no connection was ever made. Still, the celebration was splendid for all that.

There had been an announcement that Dehorter, the most famous radio reporter of the time, had rented a hot-air balloon so that he could float in the air and relay the football match play by play from the ether. But there was wind. And Dehorter drifted away.

10

Grandfather and Amelie returned to Switzerland via Geneva. They had decided on this detour through Romandy in honour of Grandfather's parents. At the border, the young pair was thoroughly checked by customs officials. The gaucho dagger wrapped in newspaper gave rise both to much discussion and admiration. The lasso made it through as a used clothesline.

The returning pair stopped in Lausanne. They rowed out on the lake and enjoyed the gentle rocking of the waves. The passengers on the commercial boats called out 'Ahoy!' and waved at the young pair.

In the afternoon, they walked up to the cathedral and, advancing between apostles and gnomes along an ascending line of royal families, they entered the dim sanctuary. The angel's wings glowed at the feet of the

Judge of the World. Only Moses, with his horns, frightened them.

A sexton drew their attention to the rose window in the transept, which dates from the thirteenth century and captures the entire world of the time in images: earth and sea, fire and air, the seasons, constellations and monsters lurking on the edges of the world, waiting to ambush men. The two lovers looked out over the city from the bell tower and the Vaud, the peaks of the Jura, the rose gardens and out across the lake back towards France, from which they had just come. There were no monsters on the horizon.

On the way back to the Lausanne train station, in the middle of the Grand Pont, even today a preferred spot for suicides, Grandfather grabbed Amelie by the waist and set her upon the chest-high bridge railing with her back to the abyss. He flung his arms tight around her calves while she, frightened and determined, buried his head in her lap with both of her hands. For a moment, they were breathless. In this position, from this dizzying height, they vowed to marry. And in a small guesthouse outside Ouchy, they celebrated their wedding night early.

As they once again strolled along the lakeshore at midnight, arms tight around each other, they thought they could hear the call of the watchman from the cathedral tower. As if he were bestowing his nightly blessing on them.

They then travelled without stopping to Bern via Fribourg and near the end of their journey, as they juddered past a newly unmanned local train station, they saw a gentleman in uniform and tie standing with a few others before the bolted sliding door of his freight shed. Two men with hunting horns escorted the grey-haired man. With one hand on his waistband and the other touching the brim of his hat, he greeted his farewell peloton. A photographer took a picture of his retirement for the local paper. They were home.

But why, Lena wondered, hadn't the Argentine become a gold prospector in Alaska, where he could have caught salmon, shot hungry bears and kept himself warm in an igloo with an Eskimo woman, instead of visiting the Bern bear pit in the summer with noisy schoolchildren and an armful of carrots.—How could he prefer a curacy to travelling along the Rio de la Plata, piloting a bush plane over the African wilderness, or hunting buffalo in New Mexico?

'Yes, "adventures" is once again a magic word,' I answered quickly and talked myself almost into a frenzy. 'Except these days, hardly anyone goes out on their own. Instead they find, as chaperone, a television programme that will offer him printed T-shirts and will follow his every action around the clock. And finally, they'll eat the bear that was killed or the locusts served up in a dish. Millions of people watch this kind of show every day.'

'What if Grandfather had at least become a stock-market speculator, if he had tried to make a quick fortune as a present-day poacher instead of trading in captured prey,' Lena insisted.

What was it that made him literally backpedal in his younger years—was it merely Amelie? Or was another factor the answer a former teacher in the seminary had given when asked for his pedagogical credo. His answer had been succinct and laconic, 'Tell stories and let stories be told.' This was all anyone needed in order to perceive and understand more clearly what one had already so cautiously experienced of the world and others. And perhaps it could also help clarify, early enough, the difference between movement and simple busyness.—'The love of and for others, there's no avoiding it' is probably the only title of nobility that real life can grant.

## 11

After his return, Grandfather created a different climate in each of his classrooms: an African climate in one, icebergs as in Patagonia in another or the blooming spring of the Wachau valley. He wanted his students to be prepared for any circumstances when they had to face reality—actual or perceived— whether at home, out shopping, before a screen, in Shanghai or in bed. They should have emergency resources that come from worlds described or worlds still waiting to be described. With such inner resources, they will never die alone or of hunger, he always said.

In winter, amaryllises cared for by the students exploded on each school bench. They raised cactuses as well. With photographs and small colour reproductions of great paintings, Grandfather opened the children's eyes to their surroundings and taught them to read images on their own.

The photograph of the young tobacco worker in Brissago should be mentioned first, Lena said, because of the camellia in her hair. As a counterpoint to her hands, stained brown with the tobacco juice, the flower near her left temple gently heightens the girl's brightness. Even so, the photographer had little time to take the picture or to chat, since the nameless beauty put her Brissago cigar down for only a second to pose, which was just as little time as her older co-worker would put down her more expensive cigar. The photographer also had to assume a piece-worker's mindset if he wanted his shots to work. And he did, aiming beyond the rapid handwork and capturing the young woman's possible expectations of a better, maybe even glamorous future. In the picture of the white-haired tobacco worker, on the other hand, he portrayed the transience of all dreams:

The old woman's gaze knows despair, pain and grief. Even the photographer's glossy picture will do nothing to alleviate her permanent exhaustion. Yet she needed her light, patterned smock to remain clean and undamaged throughout the day, so she always tied or an extra apron.

Grandfather had already come across the photographer's name once, when still a boy, shortly before the War. Theo Frey had taken photographs of twelve villages for the Swiss National Exposition of 1939. The graduating class made a pilgrimage to Zurich, almost reverently. The singularity of familiar, mundane surroundings when looked at closely made a big impression on Grandfather as a student. He was particularly struck by the language of the faces, though he could not have expressed it that way. He simply stood looking at the pictures much longer than the others.

A black-and-white picture of a young boy hung on Grandfather's classroom wall. In front of the boy was a soup bowl, around him yawned the abyss. As a child refugee from occupied France in 1944, sitting in a Zurich refugee camp, he had looked into this abyss. The boy sits with his cap on his head, leaning on his outspread arms. It's good that the charitable women in the background, wearing the sign of the Red Cross on their left upper arms, haven't made him take off his beret either for the picture or during the meal since he is still 'on-call' for duty. He knows this and Grandfather's students realized this too when they looked at the boy.

He holds his chin just above the bowl's rim, his eyes look with cautious curiosity at the photographer, who does not aim very long at the boy but quickly explains what will happen when he shoots the picture. For that, all you need is a good eye and a steady hand. And this photographer's got both, you can see that.— The child in front of the quarantine wall sees it too.

Under his work smock is a jacket; under the jacket, a cardigan; under the cardigan a shirt and tie; beneath the shirt an undershirt. Then his skin. The third picture shows a cattle trader, cattle-trader skin. On his head, a hat. In front of his belly, two calves, at his back two men wait. The contract will no doubt be made with a farmer not visible in the picture. It is the market in Lucerne. A handshake is enough.

The farmer's wife from Puttelange, like the boy, has had to come from farther away. November 1945, the War is over. The photographer must have asked this woman with a serious expression to stop for a moment and stand briefly between two bombed-out farmsteads. Overgrown cropland to the left and right. There is no expressive sky in the background of this bleak picture. The past few years have worn away this young woman's desire to pose. So she stands there. Her wicker basket is empty and her string bags are light. Is she carrying milk in the container?—The only thing that's certain is that winter is near.

Those looking at the picture are glad that the woman at least has good shoes and warm clothing, even if the layers are not as easily discernible as in the picture of the cattle market in Lucerne.—And, of course, they are not of the same quality or as exquisitely chosen as in the picture of Zurich's Limmatquai, in which a woman swathed in mohair and wool peeps at the snapping reporter. Her hands held loosely in the wide pockets of her dress, and her face thickly powdered, she resembles the white clown who dominates all others.

'Silent August' in the coalmines of Chandolin is completely different. He himself has come to resemble coal and now empties his plate. Without setting down his spoon, he looks mischievously towards the photographer. 'Push the button, already,' the assembled school children can hear him thinking, though he seems content with his hard lot and with all that there is too: bread and wine and soup, a reliable friend in the mountain and across the table. And enough coal in the rock.

The traveller in the next picture spreads out her tarot cards. She lays them out in the grass, on a patterned shawl. Her wild hair echoes the scraggly blades of grass on which she crouches. Her hand which deals and draws the cards is decorated with a ring, her arm with a silver bracelet. 'Sorrow,' she says or 'Joy!' and those on the right hand side of the picture, who have come seeking advice, either draw back or break out in incredulous laughter while behind her two boys rest under a rain fly. Maybe they're dreaming. But they are not asleep.

There is probably a medical term for the way the man's costal arch juts forward in Grandfather's largest picture. In a windowless machine room, he turns a large wheel with his hand. He takes his work seriously, as his resolute expression and his focused gaze show. Despite his advanced age, there is no sign of strain or of wrinkles. Is he pumping air for an immense organ, keeping an entire carousel moving? Or is he turning the wheel of the world? Is he one of the hands on Kafka's steamer to America? Is this man one of the damned or already one of the saved?

One must imagine Sisyphus happy, as Camus wrote. Grandfather mostly followed this advice all through his life, Lena said.—Occasionally, at the end of the school day, he would, once in a while, address the man in this photograph by his own first name.

## 12

You must aim for India, if you want to discover America one day. This is another sentence that still echoes in Lena's head. But she only recently understood what Grandfather meant when they sat together in the kitchen one Easter, dyeing and decorating eggs in a contest with the neighbours' children. Grandfather had suddenly slammed his hardboiled egg, on which he had drawn a beautiful three-masted ship with coloured pens, down on the table when none of us could meet his request that, Santa Maria!, we balance his Columbus egg on its tip. At first we were shocked, then burst into laughter and did the same with our own eggs.

More than fifty children are gathered in the one photograph that Grandfather, on his retirement from the school, had framed under glass rather than simply placed in a scrapbook. He took it with him to the nursing home. It seems the entire body of his comprehensive school in the Alpine foothills had lined up in a bid for immortality in this picture before the flying photographer.—Of course the children wouldn't have put it that way, nor would an expression like that have come from Grandfather, who had smuggled his young wife into the picture taken in front of the ark.

A lightning rod has been mounted on the schoolhouse roof against the rigours of the weather. The basement walls are damp. Maybe it's very early spring or already autumn. The girls stand bareheaded and are dressed more lightly than the boys. They all press together but are not disorderly, because they are paying attention and know how they should behave before a 'pearly gate'.

This picture, taken by a travelling photographer from Appenzell had always captivated Lena. In fact, it fascinates her even more now than before, because the photographer, without intending to, was able to capture a broad, curved perspective across the gravelled courtyard that quietly alludes to the curvature of the earth's surface.—We live and move around on an enormous sphere, Lena said, and looking at this picture always reminds her of that. And we always have the 'axis mundi' under our jackets, smocks and street clothes. The thought almost makes one dizzy.—As a child, leafing through the discarded pictures in the grey cardboard folder had always fascinated her when she visited her grandparents or looked in on her Grandfather in his classroom. As a young student, she'd always liked having a teacher she could call her own.

Several years after the death of Amelie, whom Grandfather had lovingly cared for, he chose to move from his small, single-family house into a nearby nursing home—exactly on the day the incredible news spread through the land, that three tons of bees had fallen, exhausted, from the skies.

Grandfather requested a room that faced the flat land, looking out onto the pasture of one of the few herds of mother cows in the area. At twilight, the cows can be seen from a long way off as they stand in the dark grass and seem to glow. Essentially, we're also mythical creatures, Grandfather would say now and again—hedgehogs, grasshoppers and deer born as humans. And it's up to us, for better or worse, to fashion a human life amid the fauna. Recycling, hunger, love and raising bees must be understood as our homework, every bit as much as laughing, arguing, suffering and studying. Or reading and dancing. And dying.

'Sleep well and shelter me from the wind,' Amelie said gently to her husband before going to sleep every night towards the end.——Perhaps the gravitational pull of serious illness draws one into a completely different orbit and forces one to lead an existence that seems from the outside to be hopeless and to bring only suffering, although it is, if anything, also a more intense and rich existence than one's entire life up to that point.——Grandfather used to refer to sleep as opening the floodgates.

There was brisk traffic in the catacombs of the canton hospital on the day that Amelie had to be taken down, he said. And there were convex mirrors at every intersection of the long corridors, so that death could be seen coming around the corner in time.

13

Velasquez probably painted his *Mars* in 1642. The god of war has lain down his sword and his shield and wears only a helmet on his head with the chinstrap hanging loose. Otherwise the man is naked. He sits on the edge of a bed, a blue cloth thrown over his sex. He is a tired god, an exhausted clown. Or he could be one of the local firefighters after a terrible fire. No, he's human and he's firmly resolved never again to let himself be seduced into doing something inhuman, which is what his trade as warrior is. But also not to be seduced into divinity.

A framed reproduction of the large painting hung right next to Vermeer's *Girl with a Pearl Earring* over the head of Grandfather's bed.

And, looking as if they'd come from an Edward Hopper oil painting, a farmer and his wife who had stayed on their meagre holdings would drive by his window on the way to their sloping fields, in other words, directly across from the tired warrior and the girl. The two of them would sit, upright and impassive, in the open cab of their lumbering tractor baler, staring straight ahead, past the broad, flat pastureland. The sight of them, Grandfather told Lena's mother, would always call up in his mind's eye the pampas outside Santa Fe where the Swiss emigrants had stuck their spades into the soft ground and declared, 'We will stay here.' A wider, more enormous sky arched, cloudless, over that land.

*Tell stories and let stories be told.* In fact, Grandfather explained, at this point he preferred simply to listen and continue the dialogue internally. Sometimes just reading the paper every day was enough to satisfy his need for words. In any case, according to his cautious diagnosis, there are not enough people in the world who listen. Almost everyone feels compelled to offer self-descriptions that are nothing more than rehashings of what is already known. Without any self-determination. Only in dreams do people sometimes leave their telephones behind and live, to their horror, a life without a net. Perhaps that is why they no longer value their dreams properly.——One would have to remove oneself quite literally from the world, as monks do, in order to become genuinely intimate with real life. Yes, it really is a question——and there's no other way to put it——of farting oneself free, as an alternative to worshipping the stock market and producing hot air everywhere.

At their last Christmas dinner, Grandfather remarked, that while crossing the nearby city, he could not shake the feeling that the inescapable flood of images and constant activities is nailing people's eyes to the backs of their heads or spewing back out of their sockets like slippery marbles. And so we watch one another, in doubt and mistrust, without the slightest respect for one another. But maybe it's just that the city is now in other hands.

From behind a curtain of warm air, he then watched the endless procession of shoppers for a while and it cheered him up again. It was like going to the theatre, only this time he himself was also part of the troupe of actors, just as he may as well have belonged to the local chamber of commerce which was being promoted by a model dressed as Santa Claus near the Catholic church, according to global standards.

Whenever he felt himself growing bitter and wanted to stop brooding, he simply held his breath. Of course, this only worked for brief periods, because he had to keep thinking if he did not want to suffocate on the spot. To his surprise, after such breathers, unusual, outdated words would pile up in his head, one upon the other, as if of their own volition: runnel, brain fever or turning tail, for instance. Or, just as re-energizing, the words would form up into new pairs:

The beloved and the unlived.

The silly and the sterling.

The tragic and the trusted.

The forgotten and the eaten.

The condoned and the indented.

The spoken and the despondent.

*I think, therefore I am.* But perhaps his philosophy professors in the seminary had meant something different with this frequently cited phrase. At any rate, somehow or other, after his little word and thought escapades, Grandfather felt exceptionally alive.

14

Grandfather was the first in his family to attend an institution of higher education. Had his teacher not come to his home to encourage him and, most importantly, to persuade his parents, he would never have dared. Normally, it was still the teachers' families who generated new teachers, doctors' families doctors, lawyers' families lawyers. And so at the seminary he met primarily teachers' sons who had learnt from their fathers more or less how it all worked while he had to piece it all together laboriously for himself.

What he found hardest to learn was not the subject matter but the many unwritten laws, the appropriate rituals for the elder sons, the quirks of individual teaching methods. It sometimes seemed to him that he was the only one who was unprepared. On top of that, he spoke the least accessible dialect of them all.

And if, on his frugal outings in town, the seminarian ever happened to cross students from the Gymnasium who had already begun their studies of law, of physics, or even of gynecology, and had a radiant girl from their school at their sides, the secular celibate apprentice was engulfed in a wave of pure contempt at the prospect of a crowded, sweaty classroom and modest teacher's salary.—Back at home, however, those who had stayed in the village viewed him with a kind of admiration and a hint of suspicion. But when his father died during the last year of his primary-school-teacher training, he was surprised and pleased at the unexpected consideration and support he received from all sides in the seminary. He could almost have felt at home in the former cloister.

Grandfather was invited to eat with his age group for the first dinner in the nursing home. *Witty repartee brings a certain something to every marriage, especially when one chooses not to indulge in it* was the day's motto, written in large print on the calendar for 24th January.—There were also rooms available for married couples and for new couples, the nurse informed him as she made sure that Grandfather, despite the calendar entry and the new couples, did not end up in the wrong place or feel completely lost. There was no doubt something about her open face that made him want to take it between his two aged hands had it not been unseemly.

Grandfather shook hands with the two men who sat in the parlour. But when he asked the amiable man in the tie what his name was, the man became anxious, thought, paused, smiled and said, 'My mother would know.'—The other man rubbed his middle fingers the entire time. The nurse looked at him questioningly and stroked his ganglion cyst. The 'patient' sat up and roguishly said that no, he was not in pain, but he did deserve some pity. Longing for love, even in the concrete sense, and traces of one's childhood rumble around even the most elderly bodies and hearts. Younger generations often forget this.

'Breathe!' exhorted the small woman at the far end of the table and forced air through her teeth, fiddling with her little golden purse, 'Breathe!' Grandfather thought her reminder was not out of place. When it's finally our turn, dementia is still our natural endowment and stands ready to envelop us in its dark cloak and take us away. And yet, this will presumably not be pleasant.

He was settling in well, Grandfather told his daughter over the phone after his first few days in the home. And on the previous night, he and a group of other residents, had sat, each on his own grave, and they'd had to take care of gold-plated utensils, hands, feet, nails, calipers, until he finally managed, in the dream, to convince his fellow nursing-home residents that they did not actually need to protect and care for their own graves and their unusual armature. On the contrary, they were, all of them, now free from such arduous duties and meaningless activities that so-called active life is always ready to impose on us. When they were leaving the area, a not-unfriendly woman even joined him. And arm in arm they walked along the avenue of plane trees to the heavy iron gate.

15

On his family's first visit to his new home, Grandfather received them in the front garden. He imitated birdcalls for his granddaughter and described so vividly and in such detail the birth of a calf he had watched in the field outside his window that Lena's mother soon waved him off and begged him to stop. Grandfather immediately let the amniotic fluid drain into the soil, wiped the threads of mucus and the residual blood from the field, let the calf drink in peace and warbled a blackbird call for the child.—'You see,' he said, laughing, 'grass is already growing between my shoes.'

The following visits were, indeed, regular, but were, if anything, briefer. Grandfather didn't complain, and he himself, at ever shorter intervals and as if he wanted to warn his loved ones, would gesture out towards the field where, day after day, there was something new to see or to discover. He told them that the American space station was being repaired up in outer space at the time, but he only ever saw the Big Dipper drifting across the sky and it never failed to amaze him. Or he noted, for instance, that on that day the light was so bright at noon that all the colours had drained from the geranium. His relatives soon began to consider such remarks and observations as signs that the visit was done. This suited both him and his visitors.

His daughter also occasionally came alone. When she asked about his daily routine, he would tell her about a dark red all-terrain vehicle that often stood in the front of the demolished barn next door. And when he squinted to see it more clearly, he sometimes believed he could see the old neighbour, the farmer who had emigrated, and behind him the old veterinarian in his rubber apron coming out of the new buildings that now stand near it. As if they were both coming out of the cow barn.

And, as it were already a half century in the past, he claimed he could also see Pascal as a first-grader, which, of course, he had never become, stepping out over the threshold between the two men. He wears his little red boots and the blue poncho that will soon be too short, on which Amelie had, one evening, embroidered in red thread a few things from daily life: rabbits, the sun, apples, his bicycle, his house and his sister. She knew which poncho he meant, Grandfather reminded her. Pascal wore it whenever he wanted to be prepared for anything. Up to the end.

The veterinarian pulls the thick rubber gloves off his fingers and lathers up his arms and hands with the piece of curd soap that has lain near the spigot for generations. After the doctor has rubbed his hands thoroughly dry and the farmer has lit a cigar, the three figures, farmer, veterinarian and boy, stand with arms crossed near the watering trough. You can tell they've accomplished something.

Then, Grandfather always claimed he could hear Pascal's voice outside. Maybe she could hear it too, he'd suggest, after all she is two years older than Pascal, can she hear how he calls to them from a distance, telling them how on his own he fed the mother cow six raw eggs and a piece of bread soaked in schnapps? The new calf is healthy. From his thin neck hangs the indispensable sombrero on a worn leather strap. And the metal-framed snow goggles, protection against sandstorms and wind, keep slipping down in front of his mouth as he talks.

This visitation usually ended only when the architect in charge of the conversion climbed into his claret-red Range Rover and left the construction site. A few days earlier, the last pieces of scaffolding were carted away, the courtyard was blown clean with loud droning and two potted palms posted on either side of the entrance. The first renters had already moved in, some of them with children.

16

I asked Lena if she had children. She waved her hand almost irritably. There was still plenty of time for that. I've only managed to become an uncle, I reassured her.

We looked at each other, a little embarrassed. Dessert was brought in, *coupe Denmark*. On top of the rosettes of whipped cream a pair of swans brooded.

It was only at her wedding reception, which ended up turning into a proper ball, Lena said after a while, that she set eyes on Grandfather again, having lost sight of him during her rather turbulent adolescence. The Argentine had struck her as elderly and a bit of a stranger then, surrounded by all her young friends, relatives and acquaintances.—And, strangely, not once did he appear on the slides of her childhood and teenage years.

Rather taciturn and somewhat stiff, but not unresponsive or averse to wine, he hardly moved from his table. Perhaps that, along with sheer high spirits, cheerful impishness and a few pangs of conscience about her negligence, is what brought her to invite him to dance. She'd quickly agreed with the musicians on a sign, should he unexpectedly accept her invitation. And the old gentleman actually stood, plucking a red rose from her bouquet and sticking it quickly in the left corner of his mouth. He squared his now-angular shoulders, blew his nose in his Sunday handkerchief, took a deep breath and led her, the newly married bride, to the unmistakable beat of the dance band, in a sliding, swaying, syncopated and breath-taking tango along the dance floor.

Neither she nor any of their eyewitnesses would forget it to the end of their days. It was pure rapture, pure joy.

Then the dancer asked the bandleader for his accordion and buckled it in front of his chest. He gestured for the clarinetist to accompany him in the great conga-line finale. The two of them circled the room three times, like prowling rag pickers, luring even the last guests from their seats. Then they went out into the open, criss-crossing the playing field, along the goal, side and mid-lines. They passed along walkways, crossed obstacles, and hopped in place until one or two of them grew dangerously short of breath.—At the end, Grandfather let the clarinetist lead the happy troop back into the ballroom, where he immediately returned the accordionist's instrument so that he could go back to greeting the guests.

It could be that this dance, her first and last tango with the Argentine, had sowed the seeds of her early marriage's end, or at least precipitated it, Lena mused looking out into the small dining room. That is to say, at the end of that night, her husband had seemed to her so limp and soft, leaning there against the bar, and she realized with a shock that he would never live up to the aged dancer who had returned her to the arm of her groom with perfect manners. Not just in his dancing—

she wanted to be sure I understood correctly—but in general. Even the conga line with her husband was no consolation.

Not long before Grandfather's death and after numerous separations and reconciliations, they finally filed for divorce. The divorce was not antagonistic, as they'd already agreed on using the same lawyer. Only at the very end of the formal proceedings was she able, unexpectedly, to understand once again that she had loved this man, Lena said with curious expression of amazement as the noise swelled around us. The disc jockey had begun piling it on so that, in order to hear the slightest word, we had to move closer together at the table the others had left to us alone the entire evening.

17

On the day of Grandfather's death, a news clipping from the last newspaper he had read was found on his windowsill. Beneath it was a faded photocopy of a handwritten account of his early deceased father's life and, in his own handwriting, a few other notes shedding light on his time as a gaucho along with three small pencil drawings. Drawing had always come easily to him. The sketches showed a grazing herd of cattle with a gaucho, a young couple dancing the tango and a discarded *bandoneón* with silver casing and mother-of-pearl buttons. Birdseed was strewn outside of his window.

On the record player, an LP was spinning on the innermost track. On the faded album cover was a picture of a black musician: wearing a winter hat and coat, Thelonious Monk stands at a departure gate in an airport, turning around, his arm held high, already out of range of the microphones held out towards him. His spinning wears the journalists' pencils down to stubs as he drifts further and further away, even deeper into himself. *Round Midnight*. His last solo.

The newspaper clipping Grandfather had put aside was titled 'The Birdboy' and recounted a confounding incident in Volgograd, formerly Stalingrad, involving the discovery of a seven-year-old boy had who had been completely neglected. His mother hadn't beaten him and had even given him enough to eat, but had never talked to him. He was left alone in a room filled with birds in cages and never learnt to speak. 'When you talk to him,' the woman who first found him reported, 'he chirps.' Grandfather had put an exclamation point in the margin.

And a few notes in blue ink on small sheets of graph paper about his early years in South America:

It was because of my colleagues' mockery back then in Argentina that I first became a dancer. The two weedy Germans who impatiently beat their animals called me 'Tear sac' when, sneezing and with puffy eyes, I rounded up the herd with them. We were still not gauchos, just cattle drivers who had ended up in Argentina shortly after the Second World War for different reasons.——And at that point more and more formerly influential people were arriving in that distant land after fleeing Europe. 'On humanitarian grounds' was the official justification for accepting these refugees who were, in fact, perpetrators of crimes against humanity.

One morning, I left my sidekicks behind in the dusty grassland, collected my salary from the ranch house, tied up my bundle and went back to the capital. There had always been too great a sense of disquiet and emptiness inside me whenever we loaded the cattle into freight cars at the end of a long trek, or brought them directly to slaughterhouse.

18

The El Sol was the only address I knew in this city of more than a million people. It was a dance hall a Frenchman and I once found refuge in when we arrival at port in the middle of the night. We'd got drunk on the wistful music there. Now that I'd mastered the Spanish language somewhat, I returned to El Sol, determined to take the next ship back to Europe.

*The voices that came yesterday and faded and died away, where are they now?* The singer intoned into the smoky room. The *bandoneón* breathed on the lap of a large man. He left everything up to his nimble fingers. It was as if they invented his music anew in every moment. And the musician was one with the sounds, dissolving, in turn, in the glitter of the spotlights. With his tightly clamped left hand, he led us over mountains and out again onto the pampas. The dancers out on the floor were in their element. Tango is a way of walking, the blind Borges claimed.

Perhaps my dance partner and I had gone a step too far in the attempt to get me back on track after she had said to me, 'You're the gaucho, lead me!' I got tangled up in my own boots and Mercedes caught me. This caused a brief inflammation of my skin. But most importantly, the tango virus had finally reached me. And I was infected.

Years later, during my teacher training, as I was preparing for biology class, I came across the term *tango-receptor*. This italicized word electrified me down to my toes. It is another name for our somatosensory system. And this controls the silent art of communication between two living beings, it said right there in the textbook.

'We probably think with our skin, it can rise like bread,' Mercedes had said to me after our first night together.—I had rescued her from one misfortune and was well on my way to tumbling us both into another. We made a pact. Our love, which we refused to call by that name, would last only until I became a halfway decent tango dancer—if my meagre savings didn't run out before then. And so we lived from night to night. And shared each day's shade.—I thanked Amelie again and again for her patience in short, evasive letters.

On the 15th of May 1948, I said goodbye to Mercedes who had taken care of me and led me, step by step, through the 'promenade' and the 'tango swing'. We were now dancing at a competitive level.—But I left dancing behind with her, as a pledge for our shared days and nights. I had promised Mercedes this just before I embarked and held her tight in my arms one last time.

Once the Tigre Delta had long sunk down into the ocean and the twelfth night on the high seas had fallen, I turned my heart to Amelie, completely. I was determined to spend the rest of my life sharing our early love, which had hibernated, no, rested, deep within me, and sharing our two lonelinesses as well, which no body of water would separate any longer.—Later in life, as well, I would wait for love to return: love for others, for things and, of course, love for myself too. For love will often submerge itself in order to gather strength in the depths.

The sky was filled with gold as I stood at the railing of the Belmondo and swore fidelity to Amelie. A sailor came up to me at the guardrail and put his arm around my shoulders. 'Love?' he asked. 'Yes,' I said. Later, I did not keep Mercedes a secret from Amelie.

And that is why it would be fine with me, Grandfather noted in a brief postscript, if Mercedes were informed of my death should she still be alive. He included a possible address.

19

Just that morning, Lena told me, a response to Grand-father's death notice had unexpectedly come from Argentina, written in correct German, from a grand-daughter of the deceased Mercedes, a young lawyer, it would seem from the letter heading.

Dear Family of Johann Zeiter, she wrote. We send you our heartfelt condolences upon the death of your father and grandfather—whom our family has referred to as 'The Swiss' ever since we first learnt about him. But now he has a name.

Mercedes, our mother and grandmother, followed her husband Pablo Rodriguez to the grave just ten years ago, in other words, soon after her seventieth birthday. The two of them lived together for more than forty years, in modest but not unhappy circumstances, as workers in the textile industry, then as pensioners in Buenos Aires. From their marriage came two sons and a daughter, whose daughter I am. My mother is the oldest of the three children. Her name is Juanita.

For us, a tender circle has now been closed with the death notice. One afternoon during the critical illness which would eventually cause her death, Mercedes called my mother once more to her side. With extreme urgency, it seemed, Mercedes told my mother of her brief but intense meeting with a Swiss man. This young man—as she now clearly recognizes again in the area surrounding Juanita's eyes and in the shape of her little fingernail and of her ear—was probably her father.

Pablo came to Buenos Aires from the south to find his luck in the big city shortly after departure of Johann, her European dancer, and fell in love with Mercedes immediately and married her. He simply didn't want to know anything about a possible pregnancy. And so it remained his entire life.

Her mother Juanita, the lawyer wrote, also had children from two fathers and was appalled by this dark spot in her own life. And yet, after this late confession, she recognized the utter exhaustion and great relief in the sick woman's eyes. Instead of saying anything or asking any questions, she simply pressed her cheek against her mother's. Then Mercedes fell asleep, her cheek against her daughter's.

Later, everyone decided to let the matter rest. And yet, today, it's nice to know that a loose bond has been tied across the Atlantic, she continued. And it would also be nice, of course, to be able to learn more about the life of the deceased, whom Mercedes had surely intended to honour discreetly with her daughter's name.

In this spirit and without wanting to intrude, we send friendly greetings across the deep waters of the Atlantic, especially heartfelt on the part of Juanita to her new, presumable half-sister Ursula.

Respectfully,
Domenica Rodriguez.

20

Lena stopped talking. Night fell suddenly behind the plateglass window when the floodlights were turned off after the crowd's final cheer for their team. Lena's face glowed from within. But as if waking from a profound dream, she went through the motions of smoothing her blouse and gathered herself together. She excused herself for going on so long. Still a bit dazed, I waved her apology aside.

It's not every day you lose someone and with them an entire world, I countered softly. Without further ado, she took me by the arm and led me out on the dance floor, where several couples were already spinning.

'Tango!' she cried into the room and called me to duty.

*Edenkoben, February to June 2008*